CONTENTS

Best wishes to Kelly,

Gordon Lang

Gordon Lang
THE HALF SISTER

To her with whom I fell in love at the moment of my first glimpse, and whom I shall love until the instant that I fall, as Shakespeare put it,

Into the blind pit of eternal night.

By the same author:

The Carnoustie Effect/Warfare in the 21st Century
For Führer, Folk and Fatherland
The Giftie

(in German):
Die Polen verprügeln, vols. 1&2
Das perestrojanische Pferd

The right of Gordon Lang to be identified as the author of this work has been asserted by him in accordance with the Copyright, Designs and Patents Act 1988

Gordon Lang
The Half Sister
©2011 Conflict Books, London E3
All rights reserved
2nd edition 2012
Printed in the UK 2012 by anchorprint.co.uk
ISBN 978-0-9558240-5-0

Gordon Lang

THE
HALF
SISTER

Conflict

No official papers or other prompts were available to the author, who wrote these pages entirely from memory. He apologizes to any whom he has inadequately or inaccurately interpreted,

Untouch'd or slightly handled in discourse.

I

She had wide set eyes, dimples and brown curly hair, and I fell deeply, irrevocably in love with her at first sight. She was fourteen years old.

Her blue eyed brother, if that's who he really was, had nothing in common with the girl. I had been ordered to collect two young Russians, a brother and a sister, but while the girl was indisputably a light brunette, this young man was more the type of a blond Adonis, like those Hitler Youth leaders familiar from old black and white pictures. He was nine years older than the girl, and was shepherding her with obvious concern.

The man who was bringing them could have been the father of both, or of neither. He could have been anybody's father. He was one of those nondescript types whose face one forgets the moment he is gone.

All three had British passports with the same surname: Allen. This meant nothing, of course. Possession of any passport, not just a British one, can mean no more than that a certain amount of money has changed hands.

The man spoke English with the clumsiest of accents. The young man was much better, but the girl knew only a little English.

The Wall had been up for seven years now, and it was only visitors from the West who were allowed through. How these three had reached East Berlin from Russia was mystery enough. For them to cross into the West would call for a miracle, such as three others with the same passports entering the Soviet sector of the city earlier. In theory, anyway. There were ways, we all knew, but what was it about these young people that made it worthwhile for someone to take the risks? And what was the official interest on our side?

Was it because no one believed that they would make it through that I had been selected to pick up the pair, or was it because no one else wanted to do it?

I knew the sort of thing.

'What about that young fellow of yours? What's his name? Scots chap'.

'Greig, sir'.

'Yes, Greig. Seems keen enough. About time he did some field work'.

Of course our head of station knew exactly what my name was. Vague absentmindedness was an affectation, doubtless designed to make him appear a quaint eccentric, mild and harmless. He was anything but that. As sharp as they came, he could be ruthless when circumstances called for it.

And if this job he had for me was his idea of field work, it certainly wasn't mine. Looking after a couple of young refugees was scarcely the sort of assignment that I had expected either when I joined the Service or when I was posted to Berlin. The station had more than one woman in the right age bracket to masquerade convincingly as an aunt. Yet of all the personnel available, it seemed that I was considered the ideal nursemaid. This hurt, and I was on the point of becoming resentful. Until I set eyes on the girl.

I myself was only twenty four, and still rather new to the business. Not until later did I learn that the assignment had been given me as part of my 'blooding' or breaking-in. Something simple that could not go wrong. Or if it did go wrong, it would happen on the far side of the Wall or directly at the crossing. I should not be involved. I was expected to carry off my part – safely on our side – without a hitch.

I was to pick up the pair from the East German masquerading as their father – or was he a Russian, too? – who brought them through

8

the checkpoint at the Friedrichstrasse station. That, I thought, would be straightforward enough. What I did not relish was seeing them to one of our safe houses, then staying there with the two before conducting them from West Berlin into the British zone of West Germany.

Now that I had seen the girl, these duties no longer appeared the chores that I had imagined. Had I not been sent on this job, I should cheerfully have given a year's pay to be allowed to carry them out. That's what love does to even the soberest mind. And I did believe that mine was sober. I thought myself realistic, factual and down-to-earth. Certainly I was given to cool analysis in a way that made other people frantic.

'Good Lord, Ian, I thought you Highlanders were supposed to be romantic! Have you no poetry in your soul?' was a criticism that I had encountered more than once. I usually responded with: 'I have poetry in my brain. I don't believe in souls'. This would invariably unleash a general argument about life after death. I would assert truthfully that I could not stand the thought of everlasting life. To me, the idea was a threat, not a promise.

The consequence of course was that I, the miserable so-and-so, would be left to sip my whisky alone in a corner while the others got on with enjoying themselves. Colleagues' wives, going out of their way to put me at ease, would despair.

I bore you with this only to make clear just how ridiculous was what happened to me that day. Here was I, of all people, the hard-headed, practical one, helplessly in love after no more than a sighting.

It was ludicrous, of course. I knew that it was absurd, but all the same I had fallen completely, definitely, undeniably, crazily in love with a girl of only fourteen. The feeling that swept through me was indisputable. When I looked at the girl, I had the sensation of trembling all over, while something seemed to empty my insides.

How many girlfriends had I had who were around my own age? I had one now, yet never had any inspired in me a feeling in the least like this.

I went through the handover of the pair like an automaton. The drill was simple enough. The man from the East was to bring the youngsters with him through the checkpoint at the Friedrichstrasse station and onto an S-Bahn train running into the West. The three would alight at the Lehrter station and cross to the opposite platform through the passenger tunnel running beneath the tracks. Here I would be waiting.

The Lehrter station was the first stop inside the West, and almost no one travelling westwards ever alighted there. It was like that today. No one left the train other than the three in whom we were interested. Our simple arrangement gave us a first class opportunity to check whether the three arrivals were being followed. What I did not know at the time was that one of our senior men had shadowed them across the border, not just checking that they remained unobserved, but keeping an eye on my performance as well.

It was in the otherwise uninspiring setting of the Lehrter station tunnel that I had the most significant experience of my life, the moment that would shape all that followed. This was where I saw the girl emerge round a corner, and was struck on the instant by whatever it is that strikes one when one falls headlong as I did. The girl simply took my breath away. I had never believed that one's heart actually could stand still, yet I swear that for a moment this was what I felt had happened.

The blond young man shook my hand, and within seconds was whisked away in a car with lightly tinted windows. In it were two men I recognized from our Service. I didn't have to look after both young 'Allens', after all. Changing plans without informing everyone involved was not, I hoped, typical of the Service. Not that I had any thoughts of complaint. The change suited me down to the ground.

The 'father' and the girl were to go with me in a black Opel with Berlin plates. Our driver, an expert at shaking off pursuers, set the car in motion as soon as the doors closed. He took us round and round in figures of eight, sometimes along a bank of the river Spree, occasionally through dubious housing areas.

We were not followed. Once confident of this, I stopped the driver at a taxi stand. 'Mr Allen' departed, and we set course for the safe house that had been selected for the girl.

The housekeeper in this one was a motherly type who certainly understood a teenager's need for generous feeding. Almost at once she had the girl seated before portions as large as those she served for me. My own appetite, though, had mysteriously vanished. I strove nonetheless to put down a token amount and otherwise to behave normally.

Here was a heaven-sent opportunity to practise some Russian, of which I knew very little. Yet I just sat there immersed in an all-consuming glow, inwardly enraptured and struggling to avoid what I wanted to do more than anything else: simply gaze at the girl. From time to time I ventured a secretive glance, and was elated to catch her frequently looking in my direction. The girl ate, I noticed, with immaculate manners. Sadly, these were rare enough among older people. They were astonishing in a fourteen-year-old.

The girl asked my name. When I told her that it was Greig, she announced: 'I shall call you Gregushka'. The smiles that she sent me spoke of a nature far more seasoned than her fourteen years.

This, I told myself when I was finally able to restrain my feelings, is no way to behave. You simply cannot flirt with a fourteen-year-old. I resolved to retire to bed as soon as politely feasible, and to leave care of the girl to the housekeeper. I shook hands with both before withdrawing. The girl's hand lingered in mine, while her eyes seemed to hang on me in a challenge.

I rather think that I stumbled from the room.

Our driver had sped off as soon as we two had climbed out of the Opel. It was I alone who had responsibility for the girl's safety. I lay down fully dressed on my bed and studied her documents, handed to me by 'Mr Allen'. Her British passport appeared to be flawless. I knew already that her name was Anna, and that her presumed brother was called Alexander.

As I gazed at Anna's small photograph, I reminded myself that Shakespeare's Juliet too was only just fourteen.

In the end, sense prevailed. Reflections of that kind, I knew, were pointless. I had a job to do.

That was how it all began. I, smitten with a lifelong overwhelming love and trying my ineffective best not to show it. She, unknowing and still half child.

I did not sleep that night.

Next day, as ordered, I and the girl took an ordinary British European Airways flight out of the divided city as far as Hanover. I had hoped to have a day or two in which I could have shown the girl something of West Berlin and, of course, been able to stay near her for a while longer. Yet orders were orders.

When the moment came to say goodbye to Anna at a windswept Hanover airport, I was afraid that I might wobble, even collapse. Unexpectedly, the girl stood up on tiptoes, stretched her dainty arms round my neck and stretched upwards to kiss me on both cheeks.

'Goodbye, Gregushka', she said. Before I could recover, she had climbed onto the back seat of a discreet British Army limousine, to be carried off to goodness knows where.

I felt hot tears fill my eyes, and hurried into the gentlemen's room with head down, to hide them and to wash my face.

The memory of those kisses, chaste as they were, has remained with me throughout all that has happened since. My head reminded me that the girl was Russian and that kisses on each cheek were the usual mode of greeting among her people. I should therefore read nothing into them. All the same, there had been something warm and urgent about her embrace. The small hands clasped behind my neck – surely they were not part of a routine salute.

Gregushka. I said the silly word over to myself and wallowed in the warm feeling that it gave. During quiet moments I repeated it softly to myself. In hectic times it fluttered through my mind, however hard I tried to suppress it. Visions of Anna's smile accompanied me into sleep each night, and always they said 'Gregushka'. I thought it the sweetest voice that I had ever heard, and the remembered sound of it never failed to invoke the illusion of those hands and arms twining round my neck.

All who have loved to distraction in a hopeless case will understand the ecstatic fancies with which I deluded myself, those fleeting and artificial escapes from the pains of a reality too harsh to be borne.

It was pointless and childish. At twenty four I was supposed to be grown up, and there I was behaving like a teenage schoolboy. I took a severe pull at myself and determined to expunge all thoughts of the girl.

People fell in love, but they also fell out of it, didn't they? Look at the divorces that were being granted all the time. Surely all those couples had once loved each other, hadn't they?

I should make sure that I fell out of this fixation as rapidly as possible.

There to help was my girlfriend of six months, our secretarial assistant Jill. A tall girl with long blonde hair, Jill had so far made no great demands on either my emotions or my time. I determined to intensify our relationship.

I usually took Jill out on a Friday night or in the course of a weekend. From now on I should try to devote the entire weekend to her. Friday night dinner or theatre as usual, Saturday perhaps rowing on one of Berlin's lakes or rivers; there were plenty of those to choose from. Sunday – well, something would occur to us. Perhaps I could persuade Jill to cook lunch for me. The more time I spent with Jill, the faster those silly thoughts of Anna would fade.

At first it seemed to work. Jill and I were so busy over the next few weekends, that I really began to believe that in time I might drive Anna out of my thoughts.

I might do that, but I could not keep her out of my dreams. The night came when I woke in a sweat, almost in a panic. I had been dreaming that Anna and I were together, and… well, the situation was becoming a little too cosy.

I was ashamed and rushed into the shower. I called myself every bad name that I knew. 'Paedophile' was the most moderate of the terms I used.

An hour later, when I had cooled down a little, I told myself that I was guiltless, that dreams were not conscious thoughts, that it had all happened without my will. One could not compel oneself to dream of a particular subject, nor could one force oneself not to.

Yet the shame remained.

I had never dreamed anything of the sort about Jill, never dreamed of her at all. It was obviously time to break with her. As a therapy, Jill was not working. Perhaps another girl would.

II

We have all, I do not doubt, run into unexpected difficulties when tackling something that we thought would be straightforward. Not so often do things turn out the other way round, when a task that we expected to be tricky gives us no trouble at all.

I had pictured all manner of difficulties in saying goodbye to Jill. Hysteria, threats, even moderate violence seemed to me each to be perfectly feasible. In the end, circumstances did the job for me.

I determined to end the relationship on the very next weekend. When the time came, I found myself instead tied up with a lot of paperwork and unable to see Jill at all. There was a great deal going on in Berlin just then, mostly concerned with reports of Warsaw Pact troop movements. There were signals in, signals out, signals to be decrypted, signals to encrypted, signals to be forwarded, signals to be discarded, signals to be cross-checked, signals to be filed, signals to be evaluated in the light of others. All this activity had to mean something, and there was no question of leaving my post.

Only days later, Czechoslovakia was invaded by 200,000 Warsaw Pact forces, a number quickly raised to 650,000. This tied me down for the second weekend in succession. Now there were signals of every sort flying in all directions. Jill too was, I noticed, tied up at her desk for half of that weekend.

During the third week, personnel reinforcements arrived from London. Among these was a cypher clerk who was not yet thirty, unmarried, and something of a ladies' man. On Friday morning I found a little note on my desk. In case I had any plans, Jill would be otherwise engaged over the weekend. Sorry and all that.

Not much more than a year later, Jill and the cypher clerk were married. He was posted to GCHQ, while Jill prepared for motherhood at Cheltenham.

Soviet leader Leonid Brezhnev had meanwhile justified the Czech invasion in a speech outlining what became known as the 'Brezhnev doctrine'. This effectively banned any efforts at liberalization within the countries of the Soviet bloc. It looked as though there would be plenty of tension in Central Europe for some time yet.

There was plenty going on in my life, too. Whenever I was free, I began dating German girls. A wild succession of them – seven, over the next eighteen months. They were like any average selection of girls one might meet anywhere. Some were more charming and better educated than others, some more passionate. None, though, struck any kind of spark with me, and the dreams of Anna were still there. Apart from this, I could see that nearly all the Berlin girls had their eye on marrying and the advantages that a passport out of Germany would bring. I determined to stick with whatever British prospects were available.

There was a very delightful girl I had met who worked at our Berlin consulate. Her name was Rosemary, she had a demure bearing and was sufficiently unlike Anna to be a good test of whether a spark could be struck using different material. Her father was someone significant inside British Military Headquarters at Rheindahlen. Rosemary was highly musical, and in general our tastes coincided. I began to take her to concerts, of which there was always a good selection in Berlin. These musical evenings always ended in Rosemary's apartment, where she demonstrated how misleading was the demure exterior.

We went out together – and came back inside together – for a little more than a year. I was beginning to believe that Rosemary was driving away that nonsensical obsession of mine, when it happened.

16

In an intimate moment, I murmured 'Oh Anna, Anna'.

Rosemary shot upright as though struck by a bolt of electricity. Her right arm swung, and she caught me across the side of my face with a force that I could never have imagined her to possess. 'Get out!' she shrieked. 'Get out! Anna, is it? I've known for a while that your thoughts weren't on me. Go! Go to your wretched little tart'.

Violent as had been the slap Rosemary had struck, far more powerful was the realization that she had forced on me. I had totally failed to drive Anna out of my mind. I should never drive Anna out. The fact was inescapable. I was in love with Anna. I should always be in love with Anna. There was no way to evade the truth. And that 'tart' insult roused me to almost violent wrath. Anna was an angel.

Without regret, I returned to my emotional limbo. The knowledge that I should never marry unless I married Anna, which seemed an impossibility, made it easier to resign myself to a celibate future.

To marry any woman when I was in love with another would be far more than unfair to her. It would be dishonest.

Bachelorhood did not worry me, but it seemed to bother other people. The topic was beginning to make a torture of my annual leaves at home. 'No engagement on the horizon yet?' my aunts would want to know, and even my mother, usually tact itself, would mention occasionally that other women of her age already had grandchildren.

I could tell no one either of Anna or of my resolve. It was a case of biting my lip and suppressing all temptation to delude myself with fantasies of the impossible.

Yet the unbidden dreams were still there. I saw the curling hair, I saw the dimples, I saw the smile on the mouth, I saw the sparkle in the eyes. The slender arms still crept round my neck and the murmuring lips still uttered 'Gregushka'.

By this time, another horror was plaguing me. Anna was no longer of schoolgirl age. I imagined the boys who would be clamouring to take her out. I imagined… well, what I imagined I had to fight to drive under.

When I began celebrating my birthdays alone on the Kurfürstendamm, with a filet steak and a bottle of champagne, it was assumed and rumoured that I was carrying a torch for the lost Jill. This suited me well enough, knocking on the head as it did any accusation of my being simply unsociable.

For my twenty eighth, I did go home, at my mother's express wish. All the same, I had no plans to visit Britain over Christmas that same year. This would keep me out of range of those awkward family questions. In any case, there was a chance that I might be asked to be duty officer on one or two days of the holidays, something to which I was already looking forward. To be duty officer at a time when so much was going on was something not to be missed.

'You're wanted upstairs, Ian'. This summons to the head of station meant, I supposed, orders for the eventuality of my being duty officer. The station head was a pipe smoking, benign man who never wasted words. He flipped a signal across his desk towards me.

I bent to pick it up and read that I was posted to a station in England, and should be picked up at Heathrow.

'What does it mean, sir?' I asked.

'I know no more than you, Greig. Once you have tidied up whatever you are doing here, you'd better take the rest of the time off before you go'.

That wasn't as generous as it sounded. My transfer was ordered for only two days ahead, and my 'tidying up' would occupy all of that interim.

18

The head of station dismissed me with no more than a brief handshake and 'Good luck, Greig'.

I was sorry to leave Berlin, which was unquestionably the centre of international activity at that time. It was also where I had met the only girl that I should ever love. I used the little time available before departure to visit the Lehrter station and to stand where I had stood when she rounded a corner and came into my sight for the first time. The memory rocked me off balance. I was as devotedly in love with Anna as it was possible to be. I hurried from the spot, cursing myself for the immature sentimentality of such a pilgrimage.

I had not anticipated that the flight to London would land first at Hanover. This brought another moment of poignancy, when I was required to alight for a passport check. I could not resist looking across towards the spot where Anna had passed from my sight into a British Army staff car. Why on earth, I wondered, did I insist on torturing myself?

Two hours later, the whole complement of passengers was emerging from the turboprop Viscount into a London drizzle. I was whipped through customs and passport control by a fellow officer of about my own age, who surprised me by being talkative. It was usually pretty difficult to get anything at all out of someone from another station, but this amiable chap seemed disposed to chat continually – about anything but shop.

I had long ago learned to question no one in the Service who was new to me, but I did think that this fellow might have revealed our destination. 'A nice place. You'll like it', was all that he would say. I switched our conversation back to the un-Christmas-like weather. The man could drive fast on wet roads despite talking, yet never once did he give any feeling of insecurity.

Less than half an hour after leaving Heathrow, he slowed to stop at a pair of tall iron gates leading off a country road. I had no difficulty in recognizing the discreetly secured entrance to a Service establishment well placed in isolation far from the next habitations. A guard in civilian clothes opened the gates via push button, and we turned into the drive of what looked like a mock Tudor manor house. Once inside the grounds, the fast driving mode was abandoned, and we pottered at horse carriage rate to the main door. Once my driver had seen me inside, he and the car disappeared.

Formalities were performed by a likeable, chubby man with just about the rosiest cheeks I had ever seen. 'You can leave your bag here, sir', he told me. Satisfied as to my identity (I wondered what would have happened to my driver if he had picked up the wrong man), he added: 'For your information, sir, this establishment is known as Twelvetrees'. I was thankful to know where I was. Meanwhile, the man had buzzed for an officer to collect me.

I was taken up a broad oak staircase to a room at the very top of the house. Panelled oak corridors, oak floors, oak doors, room panelled in oak, oak desk. Not much doubt what the twelve trees had been. From behind the oak desk rose the obvious head of Twelvetrees, whatever its purpose was. I was not even sure that this man was not made of oak, as well. He had the right colouring and looked solid enough to break one's hand if one were to punch him.

The broad top of his head had no hair. What was on the sides was trimmed as short as the moustache that in its faint fashion covered a heavy upper lip. Clipped moustaches of this sort had already gone out of style. This example marked the man as one still belonging in his mind to a much earlier generation. While he gave me his hand he looked at me in penetrating fashion as though searching for something special in my eyes or face.

'Sit down', he commanded. I had the impression that this man never said anything except in the style of a command. He himself resumed his seat, leaning back to study me as though I were an exhibit. I swear that it was a full minute before he spoke – a minute that I found highly embarrassing. I could do nothing but summon up

20

all my self-control and return his gaze steadily, while trying desperately not to appear insolent.

When the man finally broke the silence, it was with an unexpected half-smile. 'So you're Gregushka', he said.

Had I been standing, I should surely have rocked on my feet.

'I've heard a lot about you, Greig', went on the man of oak. 'You are a lucky fellow. We have a job for you to do that no one has been asked to do before. We have here a young lady from Russia who has made the most astounding progress in learning English. I have never seen anything like it, and everyone else agrees that she is something of a phenomenon. There is another facet to her, as well – a maturity beyond her years, and what I suppose I must call a fanaticism. I can honestly say that I have never seen such a down-to-earth, solid head on shoulders as young as hers. What we want you to do is to finish her off for us. Teach her all those things she would have learned if she had been a child growing up here. Then make a perfect young English lady out of her. Take her out round the town. Take her racing, take her to theatres, art galleries and so on. You know the sort of thing. Above all, talk with her as much as you can, and encourage her to talk to others. By the time you've finished, no one should ever suspect that she was not born and raised in England. She's such a quick learner that we've no doubt it can be done. Don't forget that there are things that every child in this country knows. Not knowing these could easily trip someone up, no matter how perfect the accent. There are things they don't teach at any finishing school. We need you to fill in the gaps. We estimate that you will need two years'.

Once again I was fixed with that penetrating scrutiny. 'I don't know what you did to her in Berlin, but it was the girl herself who insisted that you were the best person to complete her education. She is a very persuasive young lady, and I must agree that it certainly makes sense to have her working with someone with whom she is comfortable. You will be billeted here, subject to the usual leave entitlement, of course. A decent car and a generous expenses allowance will be provided for taking the girl about'.

'What about her brother?' I asked.

'Alexander? He has nothing to do with us. He is happily at large in the community, has a job with a national company, and I understand is doing very well'.

'You have abandoned him?'

'We have done enough for him already, wouldn't you say?'

'In bringing him here, you mean?'

'Precisely. We owe him nothing. In fact, it is rather the other way round. He has nothing further to expect from us. And I must tell you this, Greig. He has a different name now, and you are not to make any attempt to discover his new identity or to contact him. That is an order. Before we acquiesced in his sister's request to have you assigned here, we made thorough enquiries about your record. We understand that it is an exemplary one where the carrying out of orders is concerned. Do nothing, Greig, to impair that record. This is strictly a need-to-know operation. You will ask no questions. If you do, they will not be answered, and you may find your career terminated with some abruptness. The same applies if I learn of any improprieties. Do I make myself clear?'

'Perfectly clear, sir'. It was true enough. I had always carried out orders with scrupulous correctness. Sometimes I wondered whether this might not go down negatively on my record, whether I might not be tagged as lacking initiative, needing to be told to do every little thing.

'There's one other matter', said the Colonel. Here comes the snag, I thought. 'We have to keep the girl on a short lead. We need weekly reports on her activities and progress – more frequently than that if anything noteworthy crops up. If she gets into any kind of trouble, we need to know at once. I know it seems an awful

22

imposition, but from now on you're responsible for her. And let me tell you that if I ever hear anyone in this establishment drop any of the names Higgins, Doolittle or Pygmalion, I shall know that one of you at least has a loose tongue. That will have you out of here and out of the Service so fast that you won't know whether it is Tuesday or December'.

'I understand, sir'.

'Furthermore, I am always referred to as the Colonel. You will address me as Colonel. Whether the appellation is accurate or not need concern neither you nor anyone else. Well, I suppose you'd better meet the girl'.

III

It was the most emotional moment of my life so far. It was the occasion of which I had scarcely allowed myself to dream, and I knew that my hands were trembling.

Of course she had grown. Of course she had blossomed. To what extent, I could never have imagined.

My dearest memory, cherished and protected day and night throughout the intervening years, was the image of a slender, lively girl on the brink of beauty.

Before me now was a mature young woman radiating grace, loveliness and self-assurance in every line. She was not the Anna of my dreams. She was so much more, so much unimaginably more. How could I possibly say that there was any disappointment in the reunion? Yet I was disappointed. I knew of course that Anna would no longer need to go up on tiptoe, but I did expect her to kiss me on both cheeks as she had done before – possibly, too, to twine her hands around my neck. Instead, she took a step towards me in the serenest possible manner and extended her hand.

'How do you do, Mr Greig'.

This urbane reception was like a blow, but of course it shouldn't have been. As I took Anna's hand, which she held for only the briefest of moments, I saw that her eyes were sparkling. It was as though something inside me leaped. That sparkle was like a confidential wink. And the dimples were still there.

'As you see', put in the Colonel, 'the major part of the work has been done already. Perhaps you would like to go for a walk with Miss Allen in our grounds while your bag is taken to your room. A relaxed conversation will give you the opportunity to explore vocabulary'.

We started to the door.

'Or perhaps', came a voice from behind us, 'you would prefer to take Miss Allen for tea at one of the establishments in the vicinity. Barrett will give you a car, and he can give you tips where to go, as well'.

Barrett was the florid looking door-keeper who had taken charge of my bag. He had charge of pretty well everything else, too, it appeared. I took the car he selected for us, but I wasn't going to let him steer me to any local tea shop. I should choose where we went, and it would be well away from Twelvetrees.

I shall, as they used to say in genteel narratives, draw a veil over what happened next. It is sufficient to affirm that there was no impropriety. There was, however, a great deal of breathless whispering.

I was astonished to discover the faultlessness of Anna's English, along with the sureness of her demeanour. Surely the Colonel had understated the case when he said that the major part of the girl's education had been completed. It seemed to me to be already finished. What on earth was there for me still to do? Not that I was going to complain. Two years at Anna's side! And our outings funded by the firm!

Before I began next day, there were some points to be cleared up. 'What sort of childhood knowledge does Anna need?' I asked the Colonel. 'Hopscotch, or ballet lessons? Did she grow up on a council estate in Bolton, or…?'

'Don't worry, my boy'. This 'my boy' I found to be the Colonel's most irritating practice. 'We have a rough history worked out, and just need to fill in a few details. She was born in India, where her parents had decided to stay on after independence. Her father was a retired colonel. Her mother died while Anna was still small. Her father bought a house in Cheltenham, where he died. Luckily…'

I managed to interrupt. 'Isn't the retired colonel at Cheltenham just a trifle corny?'

There was a severe intake of breath. 'It may interest you to know that I intend to retire to Cheltenham myself. If you don't like the idea for Anna's father, you are free to choose another appropriate retirement destination – but please, not Tunbridge Wells. Wherever it is, I shall expect you to work up another background story that will hold water, and to apologize to those officers who have already spent a great deal of time and energy creating the Cheltenham one. In addition, the two of you will have to go to whatever place you choose and familiarize yourself with its topography'.

'I'm sorry, Colonel. Cheltenham, then'.

'Thank you'. The tone was icy. 'As I was about to say, luckily the place in India where Anna was born is in the middle of one of those areas that undergo massive floods from time to time. The last one destroyed the local register office – or what passed for a register office – so that there is unfortunately no record of Anna's birth or of the residence there of her parents. Pity, that. Rather than on conventional schooling, Anna's upbringing relied heavily on knowledge imparted by her father.

'We need another name, by the way. Anna Allen sounds like a cheap film star. Anna is fine, but Allen will not do at all. We need a suitable surname around which we can fit her and her father's history'.

I had my own ideas about changing Anna's surname, but it was not for her future, but for her past that we needed one.

It would be pleasant to report that Anna and I immediately embarked on a round of night clubs, race meetings and London theatres. There was, however, work to be done before this. I had accepted Cheltenham for Anna's early years. Now the Colonel settled on Swinton for her new surname. Cheltenham was not one of those small communities where everyone knew everybody else. It was a sizeable town from which many children were sent away to school. Nothing to be feared, then, from the fact that no one there would remember a young Anna Swinton.

I had an early opportunity to view Anna's other capabilities – besides her linguistic skills, I mean. I had decided that we should begin with a visit to Cheltenham, for Anna to familiarize herself with the place. The house in which she had allegedly grown up no longer existed. Along with a dozen others, it had conveniently fallen victim to a developer's housing scheme. We decided to play the part thoroughly, to have Anna behave as would a young woman who had returned to view the site of her childhood home.

I drove Anna slowly along the streets of the housing estate and stopped where she indicated. Anna stepped out onto the sidewalk, and pointed to two tall elm trees. Looking about her as though working out a distance and a direction, she gestured for me to leave the car. I joined her and looked at the trees she indicated. I followed her arm as it swept in an apparently calculated arc before settling on a modern villa probably no more than five or six years old and with those imitation Georgian details that were just becoming fashionable. We two then played out our charade, Anna obviously eager, I reluctant. Finally, I had to allow myself to be persuaded. Anna leading the way, we walked up the drive to the house Anna had selected. Playing the unwilling partner, I hung back diffidently while Anna rang the bell. The door was opened by a cheerful looking woman in her mid-twenties.

Anna had gushing off to a T. 'Oh, I'm so sorry to bother you. It looks as though your lovely house has been built on the site of my own childhood home. I just had to come to see what had replaced the old place. I must say that I envy you'.

'Really? Oh, you must come in'.

Inside five minutes we were sitting in a comfortable, well-furnished lounge with cups of tea and slices of cake in front of us.

Anna was a wonder to hear. It was the consideration of the developer in leaving those two elms that had enabled her to locate the exact house, she said. I listened fascinated to her tales of climbing those same trees as a child and even of rigging up a swing there. This was less credible, since elms were the wrong shape for swings, but Anna was not one to let such technicalities bother her. In any case, our hostess seemed oblivious to details. After twenty minutes of this sort of thing, I was myself beginning to believe that Anna really had grown up there. Twice I was alarmed, when I feared that she was talking too quickly. Whenever she did this, or when she was excited, a trace of Russian accent would come through. On this occasion, though, all was well. We departed leaving our hostess, I am sure, gratified to have had such a charming and unexpected visitor. Back in the car, once we were out of sight of the house, I stopped and gave Anna a hug. 'Darling, you were wonderful'. Anna looked into my eyes and stroked my face. 'Gregushka, will you always do that?'

'Do what?'

'Call me darling'.

I stroked her face in return. 'Of course I shall – darling'.

I drove on. That was my first declaration of what I had spent years attempting to repress.

Though at Twelvetrees Anna and I were accommodated in the same house, it was on different storeys. Anna slept upstairs, while I was given a room on the ground floor. Round the clock, Barrett or an equally alert guardian had the stairs within his view. I was fairly sure in any case that our rooms were bugged, and suspected that the same applied to the cars we used.

Anna seemed to want to know everything about me. 'Are you like your father, Gregushka?'

'I don't know. I can't remember him. My father was killed in the war'.

29

'Of course. It happened to so many'. Anna was silent for a moment. 'I don't remember mine, either, though it was after the war that he died'.

'There's something a little nasty about my father's death', I told her. 'He was shot by the French'.

'The French? Gregushka, how could such a thing happen?'

'It was Vichy French who did it. My father was in command of a small detachment guarding an oil pipeline through Syria. Vichy French were in control of Syria and attacked my father's unit. My grandfather was very bitter that it was Frenchmen who shot his only son. He would not have minded if the Germans had done it'.

'He would not have minded?'

'I'm afraid I put that clumsily. I should have said that he would have found it a lot easier to bear'.

'Was your father's name Ian, too?'

'No. Duncan'.

'Duncan Greig'.

'Actually he was Duncan Baxter-Greig'.

'Like you'.

'Not exactly like me'. I had to explain that our family were Baxter-Greigs, but that I had dropped the hyphen as soon as I became eighteen and entered on the path towards the Queen's commission. Now I was simply Ian Baxter Greig.

At school, my nickname had been Baxie. I kept that detail to myself.

'To me', said Anna, stretching across to kiss me on the cheek, 'you will always be my Gregushka'.

I was driving fairly quickly at the time, and had to change the subject.

The most difficult part of Anna's training turned out not to be the elimination of remaining traces of Russian accent. Trickier was the fact that Anna still from time to time would omit articles, coming out with some such sentence as 'We can leave car here and walk rest of way'. The absence of articles in Russian made it difficult for Anna to remember that other languages required them.

In time, this aberration too disappeared. By then, not only Anna's pronunciation but also her syntax and grammar were flawless. One of Anna's virtues was that she never failed to sound the aspiration in words such as 'when', and 'whether'. How many people did one know or meet who were as scrupulous as that? Even great classical actors could be heard omitting the aspiration.

One thing that fascinated Anna about the English language was the variety of accents with which it was spoken. The range of pronunciation she heard when sportsmen and others were interviewed on television or radio quite bemused her. She found it almost incomprehensible that there could be such a diversity of speech within an area so small as the British Isles.

Anna even tried to imitate a few of the variations that she heard, and indeed became quite good at a Yorkshire dialect (Ee, lad, it were a reet to-do) and a quite appalling Cockney (Woss eppnin?). Welsh was no problem to her, but other varieties of regional speech, such as Birmingham, Geordie and Liverpool, she could not even attempt.

There was a decidedly mischievous side to Anna. She lost little time, for example, in christening the Colonel 'his majesty'. The soubriquet, I agreed, well accorded not only with his manner of dealing with subordinates but equally with the awe in which they held him.

Delighted as I naturally was to be at Anna's side continually, there was a perpetual worry at the back of my mind. The Colonel's instructions could mean only that Anna was to be prepared for employment. The nature of this he did not specify. If Anna were, for example, to become an interpreter, she needed only her language skills polished.

Why then the creation of a childhood background? I did not in any case believe the Colonel's story of a team of officers laboriously building up her childhood history. I was sure that the Colonel himself had put this together with a few moments' thought.

All the same, the whole charade could mean only that he intended using her as an agent. The thought of this sent a chill through me, yet in the joyousness that I felt in Anna's company it was a thought very easily suppressed.

IV

Over the next months, Anna and I did everything that could have been expected of us. We were back at Cheltenham for the Gold Cup, we went to the Derby and to Ascot.

On these excursions I encouraged Anna to talk with as many other racegoers as possible.

She needed no persuasion. Anna had a natural gift of striking up conversation without excuse. Once she had uttered the first words, her natural charm did the rest. Both men and women responded to her with spontaneous warmth. It was amusing to observe the procession of middle aged men, often stout and balding, who were keen to keep the dialogue going. Always, though, Anna freed herself in the most graceful manner, and we moved on. It was not knowledge of Britain's racing scene that Anna sought to amass, but idioms. Here she was like a sponge, absorbing everything new said to her. On the drive back she would ask me the meaning of any expressions that she had not understood. It was the same with music. By great good fortune Anna and I had identical tastes. With both of us it was the romantic and lyrical that absorbed us. We went to concerts including the Proms, and I thought it advisable to teach her the words to *Land of Hope and Glory, The New Jerusalem* and *Rule, Britannia.* Anyone lacking familiarity with these could be instantly exposed as a foreigner. In this way, Anna acquired the vocabulary, and some of the knowledge, of a decently brought up young English lady.

Returning from our expeditions, we would frequently call at a tea room that had become a particular favourite of ours. It was quiet and offered an undisturbed opportunity to review all that Anna had learned that day. One late afternoon, we were at our usual window seats when a soft pattering came to our ears.

'What's that?' Anna wanted to know.

I recognized it at once. It was rain falling on the lily pads that all but covered the pond outside our window. When wind blew rain against the glass, sounds from the pond were obscured. There was no wind now, and the rainfall was gentle.

'Oh, it's a lovely sound', Anna enthused. It was certainly different from the noises that assaulted one in a town. For a minute or so I kept silent, so that she could enjoy the phenomenon.

This was what Anna could be like. In so many ways she was still almost a child, displaying her wonder at the world.

London's theatres were a rich source of the vernacular, and provided plenty of variety. I decided to avoid classical plays using archaic language, and to concentrate on works originating in the current or nineteenth centuries. All the same, Anna did need to know certain quotations that were familiar to all. These included proverbs, the outlines of some fairy tales with even the odd nursery rhyme, phrases from Churchill's wartime speeches and a certain amount from Shakespeare, such as lines from *Hamlet*. I was astonished when Anna revealed familiarity with this work. She told me that *Hamlet* was the most frequently performed play on Soviet stages. What was more, Anna now demanded a copy of the complete works, and set about reading them. When we visited *The Mousetrap* I was astounded at how quickly Anna arrived at the solution. She did so ahead of me and, I think, well ahead of almost all of the audience. This showed me yet another string to Anna's bow. At Cheltenham she had shown her talent for improvisation. Now I realized for the first time what a keen and logical mind she had – a mind evidently reinforced by a sharp intuition.

How, I wondered, had the Service been put on to her? We had talent scouts in all hostile countries (and in many friendly ones too), but it was difficult to imagine how a girl of fourteen could have come to the notice of one of these. That girl was now a lovely, sophisticated adult with a wide breadth of knowledge and the poise to enter into any company. She had become an ideal candidate for the Service.

I had been given no brief to impart social graces to Anna. All that was necessary in this direction had evidently been accomplished before I was fetched from Berlin. Anna had good manners at fourteen; by the time I met her again she had shown herself polished and gracious.

It was advanced English that I was required to teach, including that used in formal correspondence. At the other end of the spectrum, I was expected to expose her to colloquialisms by engaging her in as many conversations as possible outside the Service. Her preparation was not all horse racing and London theatres. As far as was reasonable, we travelled a great part of the country. I encouraged Anna to go into department stores and to discuss goods with sales girls. I urged her to ask policemen for directions and, before ordering in restaurants, to have lengthy and quite unnecessary discourses with waiters about almost every item on the menu. In this fashion, Anna exchanged words with a huge number of people in various situations. She must have driven many a waiter or waitress to distraction, but these were always recompensed with a generous tip. It was on such excursions that Anna was exposed to regional accents. Some of these amused her. Others left her mystified. When she failed to follow someone's speech, I of course was always at her side to act as interpreter.

It was all too good to last. I was making plans for a short trip to Norfolk when the Colonel sent for me.

'Well, my boy, you've done a great job. I don't believe anyone could have done a better'.

This was the moment I had feared, and it came much too soon. Two years, the Colonel had said – and here he was, after little more than twelve months, trying to sweeten things with his usual failed attempt at a smile.

'You've earned some leave, Greig. Take a month off. Go home. Spend a month fishing, or whatever it is you do in Argyll'.

The man knew perfectly well what I did in Argyll. Knew, too, that he had to strangle any protest at birth. 'That's an order. Barrett will give you a rail warrant for tomorrow. I suppose you'll take the sleeper. Meanwhile, as a farewell – Anna's passing out parade, if you like – why not take her out for one last time tonight?' The downright swine! He was making it sound as though he were doing us a favour.

'Of course, Colonel'. The words came out in a strangled sort of fashion. I could hardly hear them myself.

Damn it. If we were to be parted for a month, I would do our farewell in style. I took Anna up to London, and headed straight for the Savoy Grill. It was my first visit to the famous grill, which had been a favourite of Winston Churchill's. I shouldn't put it down on expenses, either. I should pay for this one myself. On my pay, such an evening was really something quite out of the question, yet with a month's separation looming, I was determined to give Anna the best.

The choking feeling that had struck me in the Colonel's office was still there. I was all but wordless in the car, and subdued at the table. To my astonishment – and, I must admit, deepening aggrievement – Anna's eyes were twinkling. I knew that look of hers. While I was devastated at our enforced parting, she was preparing to have fun.

She waited until liqueurs before springing it on me. Laying a small box on the table, she said: 'Gregushka, you have to give me this'. Her eyes were no longer mischievous, but smiling in the gentlest possible fashion. The dimples had reappeared. Anna put her hand on top of mine. 'It's an idea of his majesty's. He says that it is better for me to appear to be engaged. It will protect me from the attentions of other young men'.

36

'If I ever give you an engagement ring', I told her, 'it will be one that you have chosen and that I have bought. Where did this come from?'

'His majesty gave it to me. He said it was left over from a previous operation. The woman who wore it really was engaged, he said'.

The ring was certainly a remarkable piece of jewellery. Victorian, I thought. What seemed to be a quite massive sapphire was surrounded by a crown of diamonds.

I cursed and cursed the man in my thoughts. 'I suppose', I asked, 'that you can give it back?'

'Oh yes. In fact, I have to. Such a pity. He stressed that. *Let nothing happen to it* were his words'.

'No doubt he even wanted you to make sure that it fitted'.

'No. I did that'. Anna could be all practicality at times.

I held up the ring between thumb and forefinger. 'This ring', I said, 'is for appearance and for your protection only. If you want the real thing, then as soon as we have the opportunity, you and I will go together for me to buy you one. If that is what you really want, of course, and...'

Anna grasped my hand with both of hers. 'Why, you silly, I've just been waiting to be old enough to marry you. I've been frightened all these years that you would meet someone else. That's why I had to persuade his majesty to bring you back from Germany. Of course we must become engaged properly, not just for show. Unless, of course, we marry straight away without any engagement'.

'...I was going to say: and if they'll let us'.

Anna had no idea of the way the Service ran. To marry, I needed my chief's, that meant the Colonel's, permission. Somehow, I doubted that this permission would be forthcoming. It was apparent that Anna had been, and would be still further, groomed for a special mission or missions.

Though I did not know what these might be, marriage seemed likely to be ruled out, at least for the next few years. The Service had already invested a great deal of time and money in Anna's training. There was nothing more we could do than await his majesty's pleasure. The Colonel was not the type to let anything interfere with his plans, least of all to allow valuable personnel to be distracted.

I tried to make this clear to Anna.

She did not want to take me seriously. 'But Gregushka, this is free country'. There she went again, dropping the article, an unmistakeable sign that she was emotionally wound up. 'You can marry whenever you like. And so can I'.

'Not in the Service, I'm afraid, darling'.

'It's silly rule'. If we had been standing, I'm sure that she would have stamped her foot. In the end, I managed to calm Anna sufficiently to restore proper speech and to secure her promise not to mention marriage to the Colonel or to anyone else in the Service. She had acquiesced in the Colonel's proposal to adopt the outward signs of being engaged and that, for the time being, would have to be that.

'The man has no blood in him', Anna complained. 'We are just objects'.

As far as I was concerned, it was a damned good idea for Anna to 'appear' to be engaged. Whatever the Colonel had in store for her, she was far too attractive to be allowed loose without me at her side.

'It won't hold up for ever', I consoled her. 'It would be ridiculous for you to remain engaged, with no wedding ring and change of name, for year after year. His majesty will have to give in some time'.

This was not just a reassurance for her. It was the thought that I had to cling to, as well. In the end, I am sure, it was only this argument that secured Anna's promise to abide, for the time being, by the Colonel's rules. I slipped the ring onto her finger and kissed her hand.

'Oh sir, this is so unexpected', she simpered. The mischievousness was back. She crooked her hand. 'Just look at it'.

On her finger, the jewels indeed looked quite sensational.

Anna raised her glass. 'Here's to us'.

I lifted mine and struggled to match her smile. 'To us? What makes you think that we can count on there being an *us*? The most I'll say is: Here's all my love to you, Anna, always, wherever you may be'.

'Gregushka, you don't think I'll let them part us, do you?'

'They can do whatever they like'.

'Oh Gregushka, don't be such a pessimist'.

I thought it would be more accurate to call me a realist with premonitions – the second sight, as we called it in the Highlands. The Service could have no security objection to my being married to Anna. All the same, there was something telling me that there were special plans for her, and that I was not included. My part was over.

'When we are married', asked Anna, 'shall we come here for our wedding reception?'

'If it's just the two of us', I promised. Any function with family and friends would have to be arranged much more modestly than at the Savoy Grill.

Family. That brought my thoughts to Alexander. Would it be fair to exclude him from his sister's wedding?

'I'm not allowed to, but do you ever have any contact with your brother?' I asked, adding in haste: 'You do not need to tell me, of course'.

'He is not my brother. He's my half-brother'.

That explained the differences. 'I see. Did you grow up together?'

'Oh yes. He always took good care of me'.

So he was as good as a brother. Why should he be excluded from Anna's life? She was not yet operational, not yet even officially in the Service, so far as I understood matters.

'Alexander's father was killed while he was still quite young. My mother had been a widow for three years when she was raped'.

For some moments I was speechless. Anna saw in my face what I could not avoid thinking. 'Yes', she nodded. 'I am the result of that. One day I shall tell you about the man'.

I was far from sure that I wanted to hear about the man, and the next moment Anna had changed the subject and her mood. She was silent for a few seconds, staring at the treasure on her hand, then added: 'I don't think I shall want you to buy me another engagement ring. It will be enough just to replace this with a plain wedding ring. Unless, of course, you don't want to go through with it now that you know about me'.

I squeezed her hand in both of mine. 'Darling, how can you think such a thing? You must know, Anna, that with or without a ring I shall always, always be totally committed to you. There will never be, can never be, any other woman in the world for me. Until we can marry, since it must, this ring will serve to protect you, as his majesty decrees, from the attentions of others. And that is all'.

40

Anna bent to kiss the backs of my hands. 'Yes, Gregushka, I knew that you would stay with me whatever has happened and whatever will happen'.

At the time, I did not appreciate the significance of that 'whatever will happen'. I was too blinded by the glow of elation that enveloped me whenever I was in Anna's company. I really should have listened more carefully.

V

Since next day I was not leaving Twelvetrees until the evening, when I should head to Euston for the sleeper, I had assumed that there were still a few hours left for Anna and myself to be together.

Naturally, his majesty had thought of that. Next morning he ordered me to write a summarizing report detailing everywhere that I had been with Anna and everything that she had gained from those excursions. These matters had of course already been described in my daily reports.

Inwardly I was as furious as I was helpless. As was evidently the intention, the work took up all of the day. It was close to seven o'clock when I handed my completed report to the Colonel.

'Well done, my boy', he said, rising and reaching out his hand. 'You've more than earned your leave'.

I thought it better to waste no time, and would collect Anna at once. I packed all that I should need for a month, which was pretty well everything in my room, collected my rail warrant and asked Barrett to summon Miss Swinton.

The same man who had picked me up at Heathrow drove the two of us to Euston. After carrying my bag to the train, he was tactful enough to withdraw and remain out of sight while he waited to take Anna back to Twelvetrees. Though an emotional moment for us, our parting was in those surroundings utterly banal. How many farewells had been enacted on that railway platform – or on railway platforms all over the world? For many, in times of war, those farewells had been final.

We could count ourselves lucky. We were at least assured of seeing each other again. At Twelvetrees we could demonstrate no affection, nor was it the place to tell each other any of those things that engaged couples say. I was even forbidden to write to Anna there. For her part, in Service hands several miles from the nearest post office and letter box, she would find it impossible to send a letter to me.

Throughout the journey north, I thought only of Anna. I closed my eyes and saw her face. I fell asleep, and dreamed of her.

Those four weeks at home seemed to me more like six months. While I was fretting there, a particularly violent storm swept over Argyll. It seemed a natural accompaniment to my mood. I fished, yes. Nominally I fished, but it was no more than a matter of sitting in motionless gloom staring at the grey water. I took my clubs to our local golf links, but once only. I was too distracted to hit the ball squarely.

I tried to read, but my concentration kept wandering from the subjects on the pages to Anna. A dozen times I started letters to relatives, old school friends and ex-colleagues in Berlin. A dozen times I abandoned the effort. What could I write about, when all that was in my mind was Anna, Anna, Anna?

It was no use counting the days. I had to live as prisoners must, struggling through one day at a time. Unavoidably, though, when the final week of my leave began, I could not help beginning to count the days.

The official letter arrived with two days to go. I was posted back to Berlin, had to report there on the date when I had expected to return to Twelvetrees. My travel warrant was enclosed.

If I went south a day early, Anna and I could at least spend a day together before I had to fly off.

I raced for that night's sleeper from Glasgow, taking with me to Central Station a friend from the village who would drive my car back home.

The sleeper was misnamed. I closed my eyes, but who could sleep on the way to see his fiancée, especially when reunion was to be for only a few hours?

I could waste none of those precious moments, so took a taxi straight from Euston. Outside Twelvetrees I paid off the driver rapidly, and practically leaped to the tall iron gates.

'I'm sorry, sir', were the gateman's first words. 'I cannot admit you now that you are no longer stationed here'.

'I only want to make a quick visit to say hello', I explained. 'I'm off to Germany tonight'.

The gateman had always been particularly friendly towards Anna and myself on our almost daily excursions. Now he displayed a nature changed into armour plate.

'I'm sorry, sir. You are no longer stationed here and cannot be admitted'.

'Oh, come on', I persisted. 'You know me well enough. I just need a quick word with the Colonel before taking up my new post'. This was a lie, as no doubt too was his response.

'The Colonel is not here, sir'.

'Well, Miss Swinton, then. If I could just have a word with her'.

'Miss Swinton is not here either, sir. It is pointless to remain'.

I did not believe this, so played another card – a weak one, but true. 'In any case, I want to pick up the remainder of my things before I fly to Germany'.

'Your belongings have been packed, sir, and forwarded to Berlin Station ahead of you. As I have already said, it is pointless to remain here. If you persist in remaining, I am afraid that I shall have to summon the police'.

I knew that he did not mean police from the local village, but the Service's own security men – we called them goons – of whom there were to my knowledge three representatives inside Twelvetrees. Were I to expose myself to their attentions in an unworthy scuffle from which I should unquestionably emerge the loser, this would at the very least damage my record and very possibly result in dismissal from the Service. It would certainly prevent my ever again seeing Anna, who was securely in Service hands.

In face of this realization, I changed my manner. 'Well, if my things have gone, that's all right, then. I may as well head for the airport now. Could you possibly ring for a taxi for me, please?'

'I can do better than that for you, sir. Our drivers are all free at the moment'.

The man stepped inside his cabin, spoke only a few words on the internal phone and reappeared. 'In just a minute, sir, a car will be here for you'.

This was no exaggeration. Inside a minute a car indeed arrived at the gates. This time it was not my previous chauffeur behind the wheel, but unmistakeably one of our Service goons. The gates swung open and I took my seat. By this time, my anger was such that I did not care a hang about staying in the Service. All the same, I was quite prepared to use their car and chauffeur to take me to London. Why should I allow them to leave me standing on a country lane like some kind of beggar?

But I had no intention of going back to Berlin. I should catch that night's sleeper and return to Scotland. Then I should send in my resignation. Damn them, damn all of them!

The driver and I did not speak during that journey, but before we reached Heathrow I had come to my senses. If I wanted any chance at all of meeting Anna ever again, I had to stay in the Service. I had to go wherever I was ordered, until one day...

46

At Heathrow the driver offered me his hand. 'Sorry, mate'.

I did not feel at all matey, but the man was only carrying out orders, and in his eyes was an unmistakeable look of pity. I gave him my hand briefly. 'If to no one else', I said, 'I should have liked at least to have spoken to my pupil'.

'Miss Swinton', he assured me, 'has been moved elsewhere. Been gone three weeks. I'm sorry, sir, but I don't know where'.

Of course, he couldn't have told me even if he had known, but he sounded genuine. He leaned across towards me as I was closing my door. 'Nice girl', he called, with unbelievable understatement. 'Good luck'.

Anna gone three weeks! If that were true – and I was doubtful of it – they had sent me off for a month just to split us up. The cars we had used were almost certainly bugged, as I had suspected. In the Service, of course, nothing was sacred.

I had no wish to hang around Heathrow while seething with anger, and was lucky to be able to change my BEA flight for an earlier one.

Most of Northern Germany was overcast, and as we approached Berlin we dipped into thick cloud. I was sitting in a favourite position, at a window where I could see straight along a wing. We were banking, slowing and evidently dipping considerably, when we burst unexpectedly out of the low cloud. I was amazed to see our wingtip almost, as it seemed, brushing the side of the East German television tower at Alexanderplatz. Not over the top, but alongside the tower, some feet below the tip. I knew that we had to fly over the Eastern zone when winds forced us to approach Tempelhof from a certain direction, but could not recall ever coming in so low over the centre of any city. From where I sat, looking along the wing, it seemed that we had scraped past the television tower with no more than three or four feet to spare. Clearly the gap must have been greater, but barely missing the tower when a second earlier it had not even been visible seemed to me almost like threading a needle with the cotton moving at high speed. My admiration for BEA's pilots shot up several notches.

From Tempelhof I took a taxi straight to the Service's Berlin station. There were a couple of new faces, and two men that I had known were meanwhile retired, but the core of station personnel was still the same.

The few possessions that I had not taken home with me had arrived, enabling me to bed down in comfort in one of the duty officers' rooms. I was in no hurry to move into one of our apartments. Living alone, I should be likely to reach the edge of madness. At the station there would always be someone and something to distract me.

'Coming for a small one, Ian?'

If no one had suggested it, I should have gone out for one on my own. A few drinks were exactly what were needed in my situation. Until now, whenever I had heard someone saying that he wanted to become drunk, I had dismissed such a wish with some contempt. Though far from a teetotaller, I must confess to being something of a puritan, even a prig, where drink is concerned. I see no virtue in losing control over one's senses. Yet now, for the first time, I welcomed the possibility of emotional insensibility, or at least of numbness.

Hanson and Blackwood were two men with whom I had worked in Berlin before being posted to Twelvetrees. They took me to a bar that had been in existence for only six or seven months and so was new to me.

I liked the place at once. Liked it because it was cosy and not brash, modest rather than pretentious, and because its prices were reasonable. It was easy to see why it had quickly become a favourite haunt of my colleagues.

We were in there barely a quarter of an hour when Blackwood clapped me on the back. 'Never seen you putting them away as quickly as this, Ian. Have they been teaching you bad habits back in Blighty?'

I ignored this and ordered three refills. Blackwood was the oldest of us, due to retire in less than another six months. He had run networks in more than one country behind the Iron Curtain, and all round was the most experienced officer at Berlin station.

Hanson was something of a protégé of his. 'Never mind', he told the older man. 'Ian is conducting himself with exemplary decorum, and that is all that matters'.

'The mark of a true gentleman', Blackwood agreed. 'To drink and drink and never to go off the rails'.

That was all very well, but this was one night when I wanted to slide off the rails. Right off them. Still, I couldn't do it here. I kept pace measure for measure with the other two, and when they left I did too.

My quest for oblivion I continued with duty free whisky in the room to which I had laid claim. Alcohol on the premises was completely against the rules, but I was already so far towards my objective that I did not care. Though I passed out eventually, all I knew about it was waking next day. If anyone had opened the door while I was unconscious, the evidence of whisky lingering in the air would have betrayed my misdemeanour. Apparently no one had looked in, or if he had, he exercised discretion.

As best I could, I disguised the signs by smoking a powerful cigar. I was no smoker, but this was an emergency. Because I could not leave the evidence in the waste basket, I wrapped the empty bottle in its bag, took it out into the street and disposed of it in a public waste receptacle. Then I went for a two-mile walk to clear my head before presenting myself to the head of station.

The old man greeted me more cordially than I had expected, rather as if I were a favourite son returning from exile. This was gratifying, since in my own way I was myself rather fond of him.

'I'll not ask what dirty tricks they taught you at Twelvetrees' were almost his first words. This appeared to confirm what had seemed apparent from the first, that Twelvetrees was a specialist training institution. During my time there, Anna and I had been kept carefully away from other trainees and their tutors. Exactly what went on there I still had no idea.

I answered the old man with a smile, meaning that I was keeping everything to myself.

I seemed to be in some favour, though, since I was allocated a larger apartment than the one I had occupied before. For my first Berlin stint the Service had provided me with one room equipped with a pull-out bed, a two-bar electric fire and two electric cooking rings. The shower was an attachment to the taps of an ancient bath. This time I had a separate bedroom, a small kitchen and a bathroom with fitted shower.

'Take today off to settle in', said the old man. 'We'll see you tomorrow morning'.

Evidently I was mistakenly regarded as having been given some special skills during my posting away. The old man entrusted me at once with higher grade tasks than I was used to.

VI

It was an inspired decision to house the British Secret Service's Berlin Station in one of the city's most handsome architectural landmarks. Whoever it was who made the choice, I should like to be able to shake him by the hand and thank him.

All the same, I was now in a worse position than before. I had been able to tolerate being parted from Anna while she was still too young and I too old for her. Now, though, we were both of age and regarded ourselves as unofficially engaged. To keep us apart was monstrous. If I left the Service it seemed certain that I should never see Anna again. The only chance I had of our being reunited was to remain in harness and to maintain an exemplary record.

I had a sudden realization, put pen to paper and asked to see the old man.

'Well, Greig, what is it?'

'It's personal, sir. This is it'.

I placed on his desk a written request to be allowed to marry. Now that I was in Berlin, my chief here had the final say-so, not the Colonel. I wondered that I had not thought of this before.

The old man read it and looked up with some surprise. 'This is a bit sudden, Greig. She's not a German girl, is she?'

'Scarcely, sir. She's in the Service. Perhaps you would pass the request through'.

'Someone here? No, of course not. Couldn't be. Someone you met at Twelvetrees, I suppose'.

'As a matter of fact, sir, I had met her before I went to Twelvetrees'.

'Well, you quiet ones are always the sly ones. What station is she at? Surely you don't want to live apart. Or is she going to quit?'

'That', I told him, 'is precisely what I want to find out – where she is, I mean. Last seen by me at Twelvetrees. They should be able to tell you where she is now'.

The old man looked at me with some uncertainty. He lifted the paper before him, fiddled with it between thumb and forefinger of each hand.

I turned. 'If you would just forward my request through the proper channels, sir'.

Requests for permission to marry meant an automatic check on the prospective spouse. Were she (or he) considered doubtful, the officer had a simple choice: to marry and quit the Service or to remain in the Service and call off the wedding. Since Anna was the Service's own protégé, her suitability, I told myself, could scarcely be questioned. I thought that I was being clever, believed that this was a neat way of bypassing the Colonel's machinations.

Clever, my foot. The whole thing just shows how very immature I still was. Childish, really. Naturally, they were cleverer. All the cards were in their hands, and I was helpless.

My request went through in the routine fashion. The return signal said, so far as I can remember: Ian Baxter Greig has official consent to marry. He has the Service's compliments and best wishes. We regret that since we have no information about Miss Anna Swinton, and Greig has failed to supply any, we are unable to provide clearance in her case. Miss Swinton has not entered the Service, and to the best of our knowledge has obtained employment elsewhere.

The damned hypocritical swine! Compliments and best wishes, indeed!

In any case, I could not believe for a moment that Anna had gone elsewhere. She would not be able to. The Service would never have spent years on her training for nothing.

After that, I am afraid that I became something of a heavy drinker. I was putting away far more than was good for my liver or my health generally.

It took around six months for me to realize what damage I was doing to myself and to put the brakes on. Besides, I asked myself, what use would you be to Anna, if you are suddenly reunited with her while you are in this condition? What good is a man who spends several times more on drink than he does on food?

I am fortunate, really, in my inherited genes. Drink has little visible effect on me. None of my colleagues knew how much I was drinking, particularly since I drank only off duty and spread my patronage around a number of bars.

Just in time, I pulled myself together. A drunkard was no use to the Service, and there seemed to be more to do than ever. I was fortunate in not needing to decide to bury myself in my work. The work came of its own accord and engulfed me.

Berlin was alive with agents on both sides of the wall. We, the French, the Americans and, of course, the West Germans all ran our own men and women in the eastern sector. The Russians, East Germans, Czechs, Poles, Hungarians and others had plenty of their people planted in the West.

For the most part, agents on both sides were quietly dressed, seemingly ordinary people going about their daily work without ever displaying any political interests. Some, though, were planted in political, semi-political, quasi-political, near political and would-like-to-be-political organizations. Others were in the many groups that claimed to be non-political but were in reality Communist fronts. These last were for the most part aimed at recruiting young people by appealing to their natural idealism through slogans about peace, friendship between nations and the like. It is doubtful whether one in a thousand of those young enthusiasts knew that in the Great Soviet Encyclopaedia peace was defined as the state that would be attained once every country on earth had been swept into the Communist camp. In other words, as long as the rest of us remained non-Communist, the Moscow ringmasters would wage continual war on us – cold war for now, but hot once they believed that they could win it.

One small but growing organization in the West was pressing, without any other declared aim, for German reunification. It was beginning to attract more members and to be taken seriously. No one displayed more emotional fervour in his enmity to the Communism that kept his country divided than the association's deputy leader. This man was no rabble rouser. He did not address public meetings, but took on behind the scenes all the routine organizational tasks that no one else was eager to carry out. When he talked with others in the movement, his eyes shone with an idealistic anti-Communist passion and commitment that no one else could match. We called him Popeye, and we knew that he had been slipped into the West by the SSD, the East German security service.

I had been physically close to this man, drunk wine with him on more than one occasion. How he made his eyes gleam is a mystery to me. Biologists tell us that the eye is no more than a ball of jelly, and cannot change. Popeye could make his appear to light up like electric bulbs; he did it when expressing hatred of the things he loved, and of course devotion to those he opposed.

Popeye the great anti-Communist supplied his Red masters with details of all activities of the organization of which he was deputy leader, as well as complete information on each of its members. This did no damage to our own man on the inside. He had joined under a false name with false background and address.

Surveillance of such groups was now my concern. I had been given the task of watching over all West Berlin organizations with anything at all political about them. The men and women I sent in to such groups were all German, some of them refugees from the East who had escaped before the Wall was erected.

One woman who worked for us had crossed to the West literally on the last train to run before the border was closed and work on the Wall begun. She had seen her non-military, non-political grandfather hang himself after being cruelly ill-treated by Russian 'liberators' in 1945. Revulsion made her a lifelong anti-Communist.

This woman's history was typical. All too common, as well, was the experience of a young man who at the age of five had witnessed Red Army men repeatedly raping the women members of his family.

Naturally we subjected all refugees, and those claiming to be refugees, to the most exacting of scrutinies. All the same, there was never, and never can be, any guarantee of not being deceived. Even today I am unable to swear that one or two people we used were not working for the other side, planted on us by our opponents.

In a reshuffle of personnel some months later, we received an additional goon. These were necessary not just to protect our own people and premises but also occasionally to go in actively to deal with those from the opposition. Routinely, these men acted as doorkeepers.

'Good morning, sir', said a voice to me on the stairs one day. I returned the greeting without looking at the man who had uttered it. A few days later I stopped to identify myself inside the door, and was hailed in the same manner by the security man. I looked into the fellow's face, and he grinned. 'Don't you remember me, sir?' he asked.

Of course I did. He was one of the goons from Twelvetrees. He had never acted as my driver, but I had seen him often enough to recognize him. 'How are you?' I asked him. 'Just been posted?'

'Been here a week. First time on the door, though'. As he gave me my pass, he glanced both ways and leaned forward in the manner of one imparting confidential information. 'Dirty trick they played on you, sir, if you don't mind my saying so. Anyone could see that girl was absolutely crazy about you, so they shipped her out while you were away. Got rid of you at the same time, too, of course. They didn't want no romance messing up their plans. Crying shame, it was. We was all upset about it'.

No one was coming in or leaving the building, so I moved closer to the man. 'Any idea where they sent her? Did she come back?'

'Oh no, sir, she never come back to Twelvetrees. What we heard was that she moved to the Foreign Office'.

'The Foreign Office?'

'That's what we heard, sir'.

'Thank you'. I read the label on his left lapel. 'Thank you, Jenkins'.

This story of course could be a blind. All the same, untruthful or not, it was the only information that I had.

I had a pretty decent friend at the Foreign Office, a chap called Graham Ford. Years before, we had played cricket together, opened a few bottles together and eyed the girls together. His home details were still in my address book, and I decided on a letter rather than telephoning from Berlin. One comes to believe that every call to a number abroad is being monitored, even those from public telephones. Mail to my apartment, I believed, was certain to be checked. This occupational paranoia is what life in the Service does to one. I asked Graham to write to me at a Berlin post office.

I was allowing eight days for a return letter, so that after a week I became inwardly jumpy. By now, I was well practised at keeping my feelings submerged, so was able with reasonable ease to prevent my edginess being noticed.

Three weeks dragged by before I had Graham's reply. Did I realize, he wanted to know, how many people were employed by the Foreign Office? Nonetheless, he would persevere in his inquiries and let me know soonest. When I was back in Blighty, we must sink a few jars together. Meanwhile, I wasn't to cause too much trouble along the Wall.

I wasn't so sure about the few jars. I had already cut down my drinking far enough to cause comment. 'Signed the pledge, have we, old boy?' Blackwood wanted to know, with the, for him, obligatory clap on the shoulder.

A second letter from Graham arrived gratifyingly soon. Anna had been engaged as an interpreter/translator. She had still to pass a Civil Service examination before her future was decided. She could be posted to our Moscow embassy.

This was an appalling thought. I went at once to the head of station and asked for leave.

'Well, you're due some, that's a fact. What about that Erkner job, though?' This was a potential defector we had been nursing. 'Can Hanson take it over?'

'I'm sure he can. He's in the picture already, and I'll give him the rest before I leave'.

'Good. I'll sign your leave docket whenever you're ready'. The old man looked up. 'This wouldn't have anything to do with marrying, would it?'

'As a matter of fact, sir, that's exactly what it does have to do with'.

'Well, you're old enough and level headed enough to know what you are doing. Come and see me before you go'.

The first thing was to locate Anna. I had the offer of staying with Graham Ford while I was in London, and this I seized at once.

I waited to start my leave until Graham was able to tell me, by a prearranged pattern of ringing my number, then hanging up, that he had Anna's London address.

I handed over to Hanson what there was still to do in the Erkner affair, and went to the old man.

'Well, Greig, I wish you all the very best', he said, completing my leave docket. He reached into the centre drawer of his desk. 'This envelope contains the proceeds of a collection from your colleagues. Would you prefer to take the cash and choose your own gift, or should we buy something that we think will please you?'

I took a step backwards. 'It's very good of you all, but can we wait until I return?'

After all, we were not married yet, and his majesty might yet find a way to prevent it.

'All right, Greig, and remember: If you change your mind, you can come back earlier – as soon as you like'.

'Don't worry, sir' I assured him. 'There's no fear of changing my mind'. Yet I did fear that Anna might have changed hers. Though I scarcely dared to think of that possibility, I knew that it was always there.

German taxi drivers are not renowned for low speed driving, yet the one who took me to Tempelhof seemed to me to be deliberately dawdling. Of course he was not. It was my eagerness to see Anna that made not only that drive through the Berlin traffic but also the flight to Heathrow seem abysmally slow.

At any other time I could have relished the trip, sitting as I was at a window next to a wing, with the sky unusually clear. Once we had gained our cruising height, to look down on North Germany and the Netherlands was like opening a coloured atlas. Such perfect visibility was rare enough and should have been enjoyed, but my impatience rendered me insensible to the view.

Heathrow was busy to the extent that all the taxis on the rank disappeared, leaving me waiting, and fuming, behind a dozen other arrivals. It was nearly a half hour before I was picked up.

All the way to Graham's, I worried that he would not be home.

He was.

Anna had a flat to the north of Hyde Park. Once I had cleaned up and changed, Graham drove me there and immediately disappeared.

I found myself in one of the quarters of London favoured by students. Many of the bell pushes at the doors had handwritten names.

'Swinton' was printed. Eager as I was to ring her bell, a great fear gripped me. We had been apart so long. Perhaps Anna would not want me. It took me possibly a minute to gather sufficient courage to press the button. I had to strive to stop myself trembling.

The door was opened immediately, and a young woman of Chinese appearance came out. I took advantage by stepping inside.

I could hear a door opening just one floor up, so ignored the ground floor and sprang up the stairs. There, as I turned a corner halfway to the first floor, I saw Anna emerging from an apartment above my head.

'Gregushka!' For an instant it looked as though she would faint. Then I was there, holding her.

How long we stood in that doorway, clasped tightly in each other's arms, kissing over and over, it is impossible to say. Finally our grip loosened, and with this came the return of awareness. Without letting me go, Anna wriggled inside her apartment, pulling me in after her. 'I thought I should never see you again', she whispered. 'You did not reply to my letters'.

None had reached me, and I knew just who had ordered the interception. I clung to Anna's waist with one hand, touching her face with the other. I wanted to speak, and was dumb.

'Oh, Gregushka, have you come to marry me?' The arms went round me tightly again, the lips closed on mine and for some minutes neither of us was capable of uttering a syllable.

We broke apart, and I found that I could do little more than whisper. 'Of course I've come to marry you'.

'When, Gregushka, when?'

'As soon as you can obtain leave. And I should like us to go to my home in Scotland first, to meet my mother'.

'Yes, yes, yes, Gregushka. It will be so exciting'.

There's something of a myth about marrying in Scotland, an idea that a couple can just turn up at a church or register office and be married on the spot. This belief is very far from being accurate. Even at a register office one needs to book a date fifteen days in advance.

It was well that Anna had never heard the myth. She had no silly ideas that needed dislodging.

But did she have the right papers – birth certificate, a certified translation of this and an affidavit to the effect that she had changed her name to Swinton?

'No, Gregushka. The Colonel gave me other papers that I needed to go into the Foreign Office'. Anna opened a drawer and produced for my inspection a birth certificate supported by a declaration to the effect that Anna Swinton had been born in India but that due to *force majeure* no copy of the original birth entry was available.

'Whatever else you leave behind', I stressed, 'don't forget to pack these'.

'They will be the first things that go into my case'.

'Not in your case, darling. In your handbag, in your hand. Never let go of them. Better still, on your body'.

Before I left her – at a respectable hour, I might add – I gave Anna a note of Graham's telephone number. Graham was still up when I reached his flat, and it was not too late to drag him out for a celebratory drink.

Next morning he was away early, leaving me to drink coffee after coffee.

The telephone rang mid-morning. I leaped on it like a panther.

'So, Greig', said an unmistakeable voice, 'you intend taking my little protégé away'.

I stood motionless, felt my fingers tighten round the receiver. I seemed to have stopped breathing.

'Will you promise me one thing?' asked the Colonel. 'Will you let her return to her work?'

To be honest, it was a few moments before I knew how to answer. I had assumed that Anna would not need to work, at the Foreign Office or anywhere else. She would live with me in Berlin or wherever I was posted. And if the Service would not allow that, I should resign and find some other employment.

Then the significance of the question dawned on me. If I agreed, the Colonel would not stop us marrying, but if I said no, he would. If we could only marry, I should agree to anything. 'Yes', I practically whispered. 'Of course I shall let her carry on'.

'Good man. She takes it all very seriously, you know. Good luck, my boy'. The connection ended.

I replaced the receiver and sat down heavily. I touched my forehead and could feel the sweat that I knew had broken out at the Colonel's first words. They had this apartment bugged. How could I have been so obtuse as not to realize this? Some advertisement for the Service I am!

Ten minutes or so later, the telephone burst into my reflections. 'Gregushka, the leave is fixed. We can go away tonight'.

'What about your papers? Did you leave them in your flat?'

'No, Gregushka, they are right here with me'.

If they had not been, I should have broken into Anna's apartment myself to secure them. I did not trust the Colonel.

The day dragged by with appalling slowness. I went to Euston to buy our sleeper tickets, then tried to settle down to wait for Anna. That wait, of a few hours, seemed like two weeks.

The industrious Anna had packed her case the night before. This left me free, before the sleeper, to take her once again to the Savoy Grill. This was to make up for being unable to go there on our wedding day, when we should be in Scotland.

'No problem at all', Anna assured me when I asked about her demand for leave. 'I said for personal reasons, but they knew already'

'His majesty!' we both said together.

'We can have our honeymoon', Anna went on, 'and then I shall go back to take my examination'.

'You're serious about that?'

'Oh yes, Gregushka. I must work for Foreign Office'.

'Darling, you are doing it again'.

We both laughed, and that put the subject out of my mind for the time being. It would be some time before I began to realize just how serious Anna was.

VII

Anna was amused that I had reserved separate compartments on the sleeper.

'Gregushka, you are a prude'.

'If you knew me better, you would not think so. Let me have your papers'.

They spent the journey under my pillow.

It had been a brilliantly sunny evening when the sleeper left London. We arrived at a Glasgow battered by merciless rain. I was dismayed.

The local train on to Gourock in that kind of weather was hardly the best introduction to Scotland. Anna seemed not to notice. She snuggled against me for the entire journey, and I wondered whether her eyes were closed.

At Gourock, the conditions were brought home to her with a jolt. This was where we started our ferry voyage to Dunoon. Visibility was atrocious, while the wind was whipping the Firth of Clyde almost into a frenzy.

What should have been a crossing of around half an hour stretched out to a full fifty minutes. Again Anna snuggled into me, and I was concerned for her until remembering that in Russia she must have endured weather far worse than anything that Scotland could serve up.

My mother had driven to wait for us at Dunoon pier. The wind dropped and there was a lull in the rain as we disembarked. I became half afraid that Anna would return to her embrace-and-kiss-on-both-cheeks routine.

I need not have worried. Anna was the perfect lady with hand held out at just the right angle.

'How do you do, Mrs Greig. I am delighted to meet you'.

It amused me to see that this greeting took my mother by surprise. Goodness knows what sort of girl she had imagined from my brief telephone call announcing our arrival and impending marriage. Whatever her direst expectations had been, Anna had clearly overturned them.

'Suppose I drive, mother?'

'No, don't be silly. You two belong together in the back'. Surely my mother realized that I wanted to make the two of them sit side by side and see what came of it.

Inside a quarter of an hour we were in the house.

Having conducted Anna to her room, my mother came down with something of her familiar cat-and-cream look.

'You're a very lucky boy, Ian', she said. 'Wherever did you find such a gem? I'm sure you don't deserve her'.

'I'm sure too, Mother'. In that, I was never more serious. 'I met her in Berlin'.

That shook my mother's satisfaction. 'Oh! She's not German, is she?'

'Oh no, she's not German. She's at the Foreign Office'.

I had of course spoken truthfully, and my mother was impressed as well as relieved.

Soon the three of us were sipping sherry together, while I waited with curiosity for any slip in Anna's speech. There was none.

'Interesting weather we had on the ferry', was Anna's comment, demonstrating how well she had absorbed British understatement.

'We have a saying in Scotland', said my mother. 'If you don't like the weather, just wait ten minutes'.

'You mean that it will change?'

'Invariably'.

And it did change. An hour or so before dinner we saw the start of a beautiful summer evening. I could see what a blessing this was for my mother. I was able to take Anna out into the garden, leaving my mother free to telephone all and sundry extolling Anna's virtues.

Next morning was as beautiful as the previous day's start had been dreadful. I drove with Anna into Dunoon, where the sun set off in beautiful style the Victorian mock castle on a hill that housed the register office. The man who designed that building would surely have been delighted were he able to see Anna's joyful appreciation of his work.

All was done inside fifteen minutes, date and time for the wedding fixed.

Before we left Dunoon we ran into Colin, a man who had once done gardening for my mother, and was now in steady employment as a lorry driver. Since Colin had known me in my boyhood, so that we were by way of being old friends, I had no wish to refuse when he suggested that the three of us repair to the nearest licensed premises for a dram. After all, Anna and I did have something to celebrate.

I could see that Colin was fairly knocked over by Anna – something that could scarcely come as a surprise. As we sat and yarned, Colin asked me: 'You know that layby just before the bend at so-and-so?' I did, of course. 'Well, go twelve paces along the verge from the north end, and in the ditch, under the long grass, you'll find a bottle or two. Help yourself'.

I could see that Anna was both intrigued and entertained. She clamoured to know the details.

Colin explained that in his new work he was often called on to collect a lorry load of fifty-six-gallon casks from a malt whisky distillery and deliver these to one of the many firms producing blended whisky. I knew of course that the products of as many as two dozen different distilleries might go into one of the popular blends. I myself, having been brought up properly from the time when I first sat on my grandfather's knee to be given a taste from his glass, drank only the malt whisky from a single distillery, preferably one either in Campbeltown or on Islay. For Anna's entertainment, Colin described the method by which he extracted a bottleful from a cask in his care by an ingenious method involving a couple of hand tools, a golf tee peg and a tin of black shoe polish. 'They can never tell when just a bottle's worth, or two, is missing from fifty six gallons', he explained.

As we parted, Colin threw me a warning about his bottles in the ditch. 'Water that stuff down. It's about sixty proof'.

'What', Anna wanted to know as we were returning to my mother's, 'did he mean about watering down the whisky?'

I had to explain that in the course of five years about a quarter of the whisky in a cask would evaporate. As it did so, what remained became stronger. A fifteen years old dram could be so strong that drunk as it came from the cask it could stop the drinker's heart. This was why whisky was blended with spring water before bottling, to bring it down to the safe level of around forty per cent proof. Anna wanted to go and collect one of Colin's bottles from the ditch he had indicated. 'I should just like to taste whisky at full strength', she explained. 'Just a taste, that's all. Don't worry, Gregushka. I shouldn't be stupid enough to drink a glassful'.

However, I considered it scarcely worthy of two government servants to accept whisky of dubious provenance. 'If you really want to taste it', I told her, 'we can buy some. One or two distilleries do bottle whisky at cask strength, and it is quite legal to sell it'.

Anna came with me to buy two bottles of single malt bottled straight from the cask at sixty one per cent proof. One of these we opened. 'Now remember what I told you about whisky the first time you tasted it', I reminded her.

'Not to tip it down as with vodka, but to take only a small sip and let it dissolve on the tongue'.

'Quite right'.

Anna did exactly that, put the glass down and made a face. 'Good Lord! You Highlanders must be supermen'.

I did not deny it. After all, once we were married, she would find this out for herself.

During the next two weeks, I had to face stiff competition from my mother. While I endeavoured to spend as much time as possible showing Anna the charms of mid-Argyll, my mother tried to take her away as often as she could to show her off to her friends. It was apparent that my mother had taken the girl to her heart, and for this I was immeasurably thankful. I gave my mother the 'born in India, raised in Cheltenham' story, and my mother never queried it. Anna had passed the test that the Colonel had set her. She never called me 'Gregushka' in anyone else's hearing, and was accepted by all as a well brought up young English lady. I knew this to be the case when I overheard two of my aunts agreeing with fine Highland condescension that 'She may be English, but she's very nice, all the same'.

At first my mother made a weak attempt to protest because we were not proposing to marry in the kirk. Her effort was no more than half-hearted and had more to do, I am sure, with what other people might think rather than with what she herself believed. She knew well enough my antagonistic stance towards the self-deceptive optimism of religion, and I told her truthfully that Anna was as atheistic as I. A church wedding would be sheer hypocrisy on both our parts. My mother knew me better than to try to argue.

Where guests were concerned, I had explained truthfully that Anna's parents were dead, and added now that her other relatives were abroad and unable to travel. This was true of most, though it ignored Alexander.

Anna had chosen a modest dress in cream and burgundy for the ceremony, and I wore my kilt in the dress tartan of Clan Gregor, to which we Greigs belong.

We had the weather that every bride hopes for.

Directly after breakfast, a telegram arrived with best wishes from the Colonel. This was surprise enough, yet was topped by the delivery from him, shortly before we left for the register office, of a champagne magnum.

'Oh, the dear man!' were Anna's words. I had called him many other things in the past, cursed him so very vigorously, yet in the circumstances could now scarcely quarrel with Anna's sentiment.

We had dream weather throughout the honeymoon. We drove around the West Highlands, always as close to the shoreline as was possible.

'Oh, Gregushka', Anna called when we had reached the top of a hill, 'do stop. It's such a lovely view'. I pulled in to the side of the road. What had caught Anna's eye were the changing colours on the hillside above the opposite bank of the water below us.

'Do you see that pier down there?' I asked her.

'Yes'.

'And what about the hillside itself? Can you make out those flat tops nearly half way up?'

'Oh yes. They look man-made'.

'They are man-made, but built right in, as you see, covered with the same vegetation as all around. Now right on the top, but over there, a group of radio aerials?'

'Oh yes, Gregushka'.

I took Anna's hand. 'Well, darling, I'll tell you a story that will give you some idea of the realities of my profession. I think that you should know it before you let his majesty trap you into something you may not want to do. I was home on leave once, when three Soviet fishing vessels were reported entering the Firth of Clyde. Curious, one might think, that a Russian trawler would need to sail the entire length of the Baltic Sea, through the Kattegat and the Skagerrak, across the width of the North Sea, right round the north of Scotland, all down the Scottish West Coast and well into the Firth of Clyde before finding any fish. We had been shadowing them all the way, of course, even before they entered British waters, but since I was already in Argyll, I was ordered to come and have a look at them as well.

'Those flat parts of the hillside that you see are indeed man-made. Inside them are the built-in tanks of a NATO fuel dump. That pier down there is a tanking point for NATO warships. It carries pipes out from the tanks over the water. And those aerials on top of the hill over there belong to a NATO radio station.

'Now at night, the three Soviet fishing vessels anchored just there'.

'Close to the fuelling point and below the radio station'.

'Yes, darling, but that was not all. In the Firth at the time was a brand new British atomic submarine that had just arrived from her builders and was undergoing her initial trials. Late in the evening, news came of a pleasure cruiser sinking in the Firth. Her crew fired red distress rockets. The current swept the sinking cruiser past the three Soviet vessels. From high on a hillside, I watched as a lifeboat put out from its station – over there, you see – and local fishing vessels left that harbour in response. I watched while the cruiser, much of it already under water, drifted slowly past the Soviet trawlers, whose crews looked on and did nothing. Though putting out from a spot several times more distant from the sinking cruiser than were the Soviet vessels, it was the local men who arrived in time to save lives.

'The Soviet crews made no attempt at rescue, but watched as the last of the cruiser went down with people still on board. Eight lives were lost'.

'But Gregushka, seamen always help one another in distress. Is that not the first unwritten law of the sea?'

'Of course it is. So why do you think that on this occasion the Soviet seamen did nothing?'

Anna scarcely needed time to think. 'Obviously they did not want to take on board anyone who could see the electronic equipment they had – probably enough of it to fill all of their boats below decks. They would have equipment that could intercept signals to and from the radio station on top of the hill, as well as to and from the new nuclear submarine. They would have photographic equipment, too – lots of it – and it was better for people to drown rather than to risk their seeing any of this. Even so, one would have thought that it was possible to accommodate survivors somewhere where they would see nothing. They would not have to be on board for very long before they could be brought into harbour or handed over to a lifeboat'.

'Clever girl. There's more to it than that, though. You know what the British press is like. You can picture the headlines'.

'Indeed I can. Russian trawlermen save doomed Britons, and all that sort of thing'.

'And the television'.

'My goodness, yes'.

'So now you understand?'

Anna nodded. 'They'd be in trouble back home'.

'Yes. They would naturally have orders never to allow any outside person on board. Were they to disobey, well, you can imagine the consequences. And, darling, what I want to point out to you is that it would be exactly the same with us – except for the level of the consequences, of course'.

Anna looked at me hard for about half a minute. She sighed and took my hand. 'You mean that British fishermen would have to do the same, and watch while Russians drowned'.

'I'm afraid so, darling – if they were not real fishermen, that is'.

'I understand well enough, Gregushka. You are telling me this now to try to put me off. But I shall do whatever has to be done'.

I said no more, but drove on. That was the only time during our honeymoon that we talked shop.

Towards the end of the second week, I headed back towards my family home.

'Gregushka, I have been away for four weeks. I shall go back as Mrs Greig. They will ask me where my husband is. Must you really go back now, too?'

'I'm afraid so. We must play the game'.

And play the game we did. We parted with a great quantity of 'Gregushkas' and 'Darlings' and at least the same number of kisses.

Anna returned to the Foreign Office, and I flew off to Berlin that same morning.

Looking back now, I am astonished to realize how much time we were able to spend together over the next few years. At the time, of course, it was the weeks and months of parting that seemed to us endless.

Before setting off on our honeymoon, we had sent our thanks for the champagne to the Colonel, signing them 'Ian and Anna Greig'. When we returned, we found waiting for us a note from him. 'Be assured that if and whenever it is within my power to intervene for your happiness, I shall do so'.

He too played the game. As soon as Anna had her Civil Service examination behind her, the Colonel saw to it that she was accommodated in an apartment with more rooms than we needed – married quarters, as it were – situated on the attic floor of one of the busier department stores in the heart of London. It was accessed via a door labelled 'Private. Staff only'. Behind that door was another made of steel to which only the two of us had keys.

Without any warning, I was posted back to London. My duties were mundane, and I should have become restless had it not been for the joy of Anna's company each evening.

The department store below us had entrances on three streets. We entered and left by a different door each day, never together and always amid a group of customers. When the store was closed, we used a small side door, but always separately.

Trade negotiations with the USSR led to talk of a thaw in relations. Anna was present at an initial round of discussions in London.

She knew very well that she should not speak to me of her work, any more than I could tell her of mine. We took it for granted that our apartment was bugged, and experience had told us not to speak of confidential matters in our car, either.

When the trade talks were over, we met at a restaurant in Surrey for dinner. Anna went by Greenline bus. I drove our two-seater, making sure that neither she nor I was followed. The restaurant had a superb chef and, what was important to us, well separated tables.

'I didn't interpret between the bigwigs', Anna told me. 'I was kept in the background translating dozens of boring documents'.

Boring documents. I knew all about them. For the past couple of months I had myself been dealing only with low-grade, routine material, and was on the point of losing interest. If it would not have meant living apart from Anna, I should have agitated for a posting back to Berlin, or to anywhere with plenty of activity.

Not a fortnight later, Anna announced that she was to go with a British trade delegation to Moscow.

'Anna!'

'It's all right, Gregushka'.

It was true that she had meanwhile been naturalized and would have accreditation as a member of the Foreign Office mission. All the same, I was concerned. Did she really have to enter the lions' den?

'Darling', I told her 'I doubt that you will be identified as a schoolgirl who went missing years ago and is probably presumed dead. That's not what worries me. It's that they will soon know who Anna Greig's husband is – if they don't know already, which they probably do. They must suppose that you will pass on to me any intelligence that comes your way. It would be absurd not to assume this, and it is likely to put you into the position of being closely watched everywhere you go. You may find your stay there very uncomfortable'.

Of course, the same applied to every member of the British mission. It was not necessary to have a spouse in the Service to be regarded with suspicion. Marriage to me made Anna perhaps no more dangerous in Soviet eyes than was anyone else. Trade missions, theirs the same as ours, always included espionage specialists. They did it to us, and we did it to them. Both sides knew it.

All the same, none of these considerations stopped me biting my nails, figuratively of course, all the time that Anna was away. For the first time, I began to appreciate the benefit of having a dull posting with undemanding work. Had I still been in Berlin, running agents in the East, I should have found the sheer worry about Anna interfering with the concentration required for my work. An officer with too much on his mind is a danger to the Service.

On Anna's return, we met again for dinner, but this time at a different restaurant. I was anxious to avoid establishing any kind of routine.

'The same old stuff', said Anna. 'Translating documents. It's very funny, really, what I've been doing, because interpreters translate best into their own native languages. That's why you'll see two interpreters at these talks. A Russian interpreter tells the Russian negotiator what the British representative has said, and vice versa. It's the same with written translations. We can all translate both ways, but we do it better into our own native languages. It should be a British girl doing what I do, putting Russian into English. That's the joke'.

'But you can do it as though English were your native language, Anna. You're an absolute marvel'.

Even so, I could not help wishing that she were not quite so good. Only ten days later, she was off to Moscow with the British delegation once again.

'Just the same', she reported. 'Paperwork'.

Outside our attic flat there had once been a roof garden. Brick walls eighteen inches high held what had been raised flower beds. All was now in disrepair, so while Anna was away I converted the bed nearest to our windows into a pond. I had most of the soil removed and the brickwork sealed, then filled the construction with water. I planted both pink and white water lilies.

As intended, Anna on her return was delighted with the result. While she longed to hear rain pattering on the lily pads, London had made up its mind to inflict on its inhabitants a prolonged dry spell. The rain came eventually, of course, and when it did, it was far too much. If that isn't British weather in a nutshell, I don't know what is.

74

It was nearly a year before a further Soviet mission arrived in London. This time, Anna told me with some satisfaction that there had been no paperwork to translate. She had acted as interpreter between some of the lesser figures on each side. 'It was fun', she summarized.

Barely two months later, she was off again. Brezhnev was seeking détente, and it was easy to see why. Under his rule, the USSR had stagnated. Military expenditure had long been the dead weight dragging down the Soviet economy. Russia could not match the tremendous pace of technological advances in the West. With enormous effort, the Soviet Union would pull itself forwards a single step, only to find that meanwhile the West had moved on two or three strides farther ahead. It was a never ending game of catch-me-if-you-can, in which Russia became progressively weakened and doomed always to lag behind.

Only if the Western powers could be persuaded that there was no real threat to them would they relax their efforts, allowing the Soviet Union a breathing space.

This was the thinking behind Brezhnev's moves towards détente. Its aim was to persuade the West to apply the brakes in the endless race between the two blocs.

VIII

Really, I should have seen it coming. The Colonel had some purpose in mind for Anna. His efforts to keep me away from her had made that clear. I had imagined that, with missions going backwards and forwards, either Russian or our own, she was expected to pick up whatever was to be picked up in the course of interpreting and translation. I had been warned, yet not taken seriously that she would be posted to our Moscow Embassy permanently.

'No need to worry, Gregushka', she told me over and over.

I worried, just the same. I had been tense throughout each of her visits to Moscow when these had lasted only a few days. I was going to be in a worse state thinking of her being there all the time.

'Gregushka, I shall have diplomatic immunity. If they take exception to me, the most they can do is throw me out of the country'.

This was true enough. All the same, I disliked the idea of her posting from the beginning.

With Anna absent from what of necessity had become our London home, I applied at once for a posting back to Berlin. This was granted with such speed that it threw up a disturbing line of thought. It looked as though Anna had been intended for Moscow all along, with our brief time in London merely a sort of extended honeymoon, courtesy of the Service, before the planned parting. It was certainly true that my request was processed with unprecedented rapidity. I was on a plane for Tempelhof two days after seeing off Anna at Heathrow.

Among the agents whom I now partly controlled in the Soviet zone was a senior East German official who had the code name of Mustard. This was a man in good standing with the Russians. He made frequent trips to Moscow and had been recruited by their service before beginning to work for us. As far as I am aware, Mustard was the most highly placed double agent that we had. He was certainly the most important outside the USSR itself.

Over the years he provided us not just with detailed information about arms production and military planning. Most important was his guide to Soviet thinking. His own government did not count; all that mattered was what Moscow decreed. Mustard had sat in at many policy-making meetings. Even when he had not been present at a conference, he was there when the orders came down, and so was always abreast of what had been decided.

To know what the other fellow thought was frequently more important than knowing what he was doing. In this respect, Mustard was an absolute gift. This was why he was such a critical loss to us when he came across to the West. Mustard was the sort of agent any service would want to have in the other fellow's camp. Once he defects, his usefulness is limited chiefly to what he knows up to the time of his defection. He can still interpret the intention behind moves by the other side, but as an ongoing source, he is lost.

A postcard to a private address in West Berlin told us that Mustard wanted to come over to us. It bore a picture of the Baltic island of Rügen, playground of East German party members and favoured officials. Its written message concerned only the weather. This was Mustard's alarm signal, telling us that the SSD was on to him. We took him out via a roundabout route. Since the man was too nervous for debriefing even when safely on West German soil, I flew with him to London. I could see that he would relax properly only once we had him in Britain.

As it turned out, the most valuable things he had to tell us concerned personalities rather than military preparedness. Thanks in no small part to Mustard's own work, we were already well informed of all the latest Warsaw Pact developments. There was little to surprise us.

We knew what the Warsaw Pact leadership considered to be the weaknesses in NATO and the advantages enjoyed by its own forces. In Moscow they justifiably counted as their advantage the fact that in war they would operate from a single territorial mass having great depth, unbroken by natural obstacles. They had convenient conditions for supplies by land, air, sea and river; enjoyed a high level of standardization of equipment and could mobilize twenty per cent of Warsaw Pact populations, against NATO's twelve per cent.

A principal weakness in NATO they identified in the difficulty, cost and vulnerability of fuel transport. For every ton of petrol delivered from America to Western Europe by air, tanker aircraft would on average themselves consume another ton of fuel. A tanker bringing fuel from the Middle East by sea would require twenty five to thirty days, since the Suez Canal could easily be blocked and pipelines through countries such as Syria blown up. Furthermore, NATO forces had little standardization of weapons and equipment.

These unarguable facts were sufficient to give Warsaw Pact leaders confidence in all negotiations with the West. The question was whether they trusted in their advantages sufficiently to take any risks.

Where giving insights into the Moscow mentality was concerned, Mustard was a minor goldmine. Among other matters, he confirmed something of which we already had indications: that Brezhnev did not act as a lone dictator but made all decisions only after consulting his Central Committee colleagues. This was in direct contrast to his predecessor Khrushchev, who had perhaps been ousted precisely because he acted alone. Undoubtedly, these matters would surprise the public in western countries. The man in the street seems to have seen Khrushchev as a rather jovial figure, whereas Brezhnev appeared forbidding.

Mustard had plenty to tell us of the determining mood in Moscow, of the Kremlin's caution in foreign policy, its concern about dwindling party membership in the West and its efforts to increase subversion in Africa. Mustard had attended receptions at the Moscow Foreign Ministry as well as at several foreign embassies there.

'This straight line they have into Whitehall', Mustard asked, 'is that another one of your double agents?'

'Into Whitehall where?'

'The Foreign Office'.

I had some difficulty in getting the words out. 'You mean they've planted an agent in the Foreign Office?'

'Didn't need to. She came to them'.

I felt sick. 'She?'

'Oh yes. A most attractive young lady'.

'What is her position at the Foreign Office? Do you know?'

'Translator. Remarkably good, too. Everyone says she's the best they've ever encountered. She's at all the receptions. A big favourite of all the leading Russians'.

'Can you give us a description?'

'Brown curly hair, wide set blue eyes – and dimples. Most attractive dimples'.

'Could you identify her from a photograph?'

'Oh yes. No question. She has a face no one would ever forget. A real beauty. Such a pity that she will have to end in prison, either yours or theirs'. He sighed. 'And if it's theirs, it could be worse than prison'.

I stopped the interview right there. I could not go on.

Apart from feeling as sick as I had ever been, I knew that if I didn't take the matter higher, Mustard was sure to tell someone else.

I took it at once to the chief of the Service, and found myself detained. A resident goon placed me hands to the wall and frisked me for the weapon that was not there.

That night was the worst I had ever spent, and not because I was kept in a small room with a goon for company. Anna working for Moscow? It was unthinkable. Yet I could not help remembering Popeye, the apparently fanatical anti-Communist who had fooled the West Germans.

Mustard said that it was Anna who had made the approach to Moscow. Impossible to imagine – yet whoever had moved first, it must have been a recent contact. They couldn't possibly have planted Anna on us when she was only fourteen.

I had always made fun of those who claimed that spiritual or mental anguish was worse than physical pain. I have taken a bullet, and know just a little about bodily hurt. Yet that night I was prepared to concede that mental distress, while not a direct pain, could after all weaken a man just as comprehensively. By the time I was escorted to the chief next day, I was thoroughly worn out. All the same, I was determined to defend Anna against all comers.

The chief wasted no time. 'Right, Greig, you are suspended as of now. You may well find yourself facing criminal charges. Your wife has been positively identified from her photograph and will be returned to the UK at once. Meanwhile, you will be placed under house arrest while we establish the level of your complicity in your wife's conduct'.

Two goons whipped me out of there faster than they had taken me in. They marched me to an interrogation room and stood over me while I waited until the head of Russia Section should be graciously pleased to appear.

In he came after half an hour, taking his seat opposite me flanked by two acolytes. At any other time I should have found the man's self-important pose comical. Now I was scarcely in condition to find any humour in his pretensions to be a presiding Nemesis.

'Who was the first to start working for the KGB? You or your wife?'

'We know that your wife volunteered her services to them. Did you volunteer yours, or did they approach you?'

'When did your wife tell you that she was working for the KGB?'

'When did you begin helping her?'

'Did she recruit you, or did you recruit her?'

'Were you working for the KGB first?'

'Who is your KGB controller?'

'Is he here in London? Or in Berlin? Do you cross through into the East to report and receive your pay?'

'Who is your wife's controller?'

'Did your controller order you to recruit your wife?'

'How do they pay you?'

'How much is each of you paid?'

'How do you pass on the information when you're in London?'

'Have they given you any medals yet? The Order of Lenin, perhaps? Or the Order of the Red Banner?'

'What medals has your wife received?'

'What currency do they pay you in? Sterling, or dollars? You surely don't let them fob you off with roubles'.

'How did you first make contact? Or did they come to you?'

'What hold do they have over you? Or didn't they need one? An idealist, are you? Wanting to make your contribution to building the brave new socialist world?'

'What could they blackmail you with? Some indiscretion in Berlin, was it? Or here? What was the name of the woman? Wasn't a boy, was it?'

'Were you already on the KGB payroll when you picked up your wife and her brother in Berlin?'

'When did you become a Communist?'

'Were you already a Communist when you joined this Service, or did she convert you?'

'What is the name of your controller?'

'Does your wife have the same controller?'

On and on. The same inane questions over and over.

I knew the system as well as they did. Keep on firing questions until the suspect can take no more. Take turns in the room, so that the interrogators can have some sleep, but don't let the suspect snatch any. Wear him down.

I already had a sleepless night behind me. It was going to be easier for them to push me over the edge. Yet I had to keep awake and aggressive in my responses. It's a guilty suspect who quietens down as the questioning goes on. An innocent man will become angrier and angrier.

I was angry enough already. I cursed them for a pack of bloody fools. I threw at them everything I could think of, flung in their faces all Russia Section's mistakes that were common knowledge throughout the Service.

The section head went white. For a moment I thought that one of his devotees was going to spring out of his seat and attack me.

'Let's leave it at that for now, shall we?' ordered the section head. The three men rose and left. By the disciples, I was treated to ugly looks. The white-faced section head remained expressionless. A slender man with large ears, he had a natural dignity that was impressive even under these circumstances of hostility.

What was really making me so very angry was not so much my being subjected to false accusations as the thought of Anna's being treated in similar fashion.

A pair of office goons took me to a spare, windowless room used by overnight duty officers, removed the television and radio sets and locked me in with silent sneers. I had a bed of sorts – the folding kind – and a small table. My watch had not been taken, so I knew that it was midnight before the door opened. A female member of staff came in carrying a tray with tea and two sandwiches. She placed it on the table, avoided looking at me, and left without a word.

It was not difficult to guess that everyone was forbidden to speak to me. In the Service, quaint ideas such as being treated as innocent until proven guilty were, and are, unknown.

I had expected another sleepless night, and was wrong. I not only slept but dreamed. It was usual for me to dream of Anna, not just when we were parted but even when she was in our bed beside me. Now I dreamed of her in a dungeon that metamorphosed into a courtroom where no one would listen to her.

I woke believing that it was all real and knowing that I had to get over to that courtroom as fast as possible. I started to climb from the bed. Then reality caught up with me and I sank back.

Probably Anna was already in Britain. Or was she still on the way?

One thing was certain. They would not let us see one another.

Twice that day a woman brought in food and drink, and twice that day a goon escorted me to a lavatory on the same floor. I spent the hours between worrying about Anna.

The door did not open again until nearly seven in the evening.

In the doorway stood the Colonel. A furious look was on his face. 'My dear chap', he said. 'For goodness' sake come out of there at once'.

The furious look was directed not at me, but at the goon who had opened the door.

IX

Within five minutes I was seated beside the Colonel in an unobtrusive Rover that he was driving himself.

'Where', I demanded, 'is Anna?'

'You mean at this minute?'

'Yes'.

'Don't worry. As far as I know she's at our embassy in Moscow. She's certainly in Moscow still. As soon as I heard this nonsense about bringing her back, I put a stop to it. And don't worry. No one at the embassy knows anything about these ridiculous suspicions'.

Except your man there, I thought.

The next minutes of our journey the Colonel spent cursing the alleged obtuseness of everyone at headquarters. While he was doing so, I could not help thinking that his vituperation was fuelled rather by the frustrations of London's traffic than by any justified complaint against our superiors.

Even to an outsider it would be apparent that the Chief could have done no other than treat me as suspect. Husband and wife teams were relatively frequent in KGB networks. The fact that I had reported what Mustard told me about Anna was meaningless. It would have looked ten times worse for me had I kept it quiet, only for Mustard later to tell another officer that he had put me in the picture. My going directly to the Chief must appear an obvious attempt to cover my own position.

The Colonel knew all this, and I knew it.

'Ten years' work damned nearly blown sky high', he complained.

Ten years! That meant that he had planned to use Anna all along. I turned on him. 'Not so, my dear chap', he insisted. 'No. It was the boy we wanted. Alexander. The girl was just window dressing'.

That made me just as angry. 'What do you mean, window dressing?'

'She was cover for Alexander coming across. Better a young brother and sister than a man of military age on his own'.

'But why on earth did you want Alexander? He was only twenty three at the time'.

'The lad had been a cypher clerk for five years. He got in touch with us eighteen months before he came over here. The stuff he was sending us was gold, pure gold. Then things started to become hot, and we had to get him out. It was their mother who wanted us to bring the girl over as well, and as it happened that made perfect sense. As I said, beautiful cover for the crossing rather than a young man on his own'.

'And he's working for us now?'

'Working for me. A cypher specialist'.

Despite my relief that Anna had been spared interrogation, I was still angry that she had been dragged in to the Service at all. 'You'd been meaning to recruit her all along, hadn't you?' I challenged.

'Not at all. Not until we saw how well she had developed. It was you who brought out her latent capabilities'.

'But you mentioned ten years' work. It's ten years since she and Alexander came over. You must have been planning and preparing to use her from the start'.

'Ten years, I admit, was an exaggeration. Not an exaggeration in Alexander's case, but as far as Anna is concerned, yes. Anyway, you must agree that she was practically a gift – a perfect Russian speaker, fanatical in her hatred of the régime. Admittedly, we didn't know her feelings at the outset. All we knew was that her mother wanted her out of there. It was more or less a package deal. If we wanted Alexander, we had to take the girl as well. What would you have done?'

'And the chap who acted as their father?'

'He was not one of ours. An escape helper. He did it just for the money. There are lots like him'.

That was what I had supposed. 'You said that Alexander is working for you rather than for the Service'.

'That's a little misleading. Naturally, in working for me he's working for the Service, but what we are at Twelvetrees is a special division, an offshoot if you like. We do all the nasty jobs that are even nastier than the ones they do in all the other departments. We also specialize in running double agents'.

'And that's what Anna is?'

'She will be in time. The truth is that Mustard had got hold of a story that is only half true. He broke the first rule for any agent'.

'Not to turn in information before he has made the best attempt he can to check it out'.

'Exactly. Yes, Anna is very popular in Moscow, and yes, the KGB has been taking an interest in her, but no, she has not started working for them. They are still just sizing her up. Someone was simply trying to impress Mustard with nonsensical loose-tongued bragging. It is entirely without foundation, I assure you. If they do recruit Anna, she will immediately report that fact to us'.

'Does she have any say?'

'Of course. No one is compelling her to do anything. And just like yourself she can leave the Service at any time'.

Apart from that initial burst of anger when the Colonel had tried to split up the two of us, I had never considered resigning. In all honesty, I had never imagined that a time could come when I should want to leave. Now it seemed that in order to protect Anna, resignation might be the best course for both of us.

It was as though the Colonel knew what I was thinking. He actually smiled. That is, half smiled. I never did see him smile fully, and even his half smiles were rare, nothing more than a controlled widening of the lips, as though the man did not trust himself not to lose his self-control.

'Cheer up, my lad. This is a war we are in, and you want to be around when we win it, don't you? And don't forget: so far as Anna is concerned, she is protected by her diplomatic status'.

I was scarcely reassured by this, any more than I was prepared for what came next. 'How would you like to join me at Twelvetrees? Always plenty to do. Train a few newcomers, for example. You can run one or two doubles, as well – except Anna, of course. She is my province'.

This astonished me so much that I did not respond at once.

'Come on, lad', urged the Colonel. 'Is it so wonderful in Berlin?'

'It's the front line'.

'Ah. Of course. Where you young fellows always want to be. Tell you what. How would it be if I tell your head of station to give you a month's leave, and do the same for Anna? You can go away somewhere together and talk it over between you. Then when the month is up Anna will go back to Moscow and you can decide whether to carry on with your routine work in Berlin or start on the exciting path with us at Twelvetrees'.

'You couldn't be more impartial if you tried, could you?'

'My boy, I know these outstations, and the jiggery-pokery that goes on there. You were lucky with Mustard, but when do you think another one like him will turn up? And if he does, will they let you handle him, or will some senior chap hog him all to himself?'

90

'I had Mustard all to myself'.

'That's because you found him, and the station was short of personnel at the time. It won't happen again, take my word for it. There's too much jealousy around. At Twelvetrees you will find yourself tackling challenging and exciting jobs all the time'.

Challenging and exciting? Training recruits, he had said. This might prove challenging enough if the rookies were not up to scratch, but surely it could never be exciting.

All the same, the Colonel's offer was convenient. If Anna were soon to arrive in London, there was no point in my flying back to Berlin. In any case, Berlin goons would have pulled apart my rooms there, just as others would have torn our London apartment to pieces. They would have been looking for a radio transmitter or any other paraphernalia to convict Anna and me of working for the opposition.

I knew the mess they would have left behind, and had no wish to see it. I had no desire to see anyone from Headquarters, either.

In consequence, I stayed in the Rover all the way to Twelvetrees – without prejudice, as I made clear. I would go on a month's leave as suggested. Meanwhile, the Colonel instructed Barrett to give me a larger room than I had occupied before.

The Colonel was a marvel. He twisted the chief's arm sufficiently to force the detailing of goons to put everything back in order in both apartments. In London they did it under my supervision.

The job was completed before Anna landed at Heathrow two days later.

To my surprise, the Colonel gave me no further sales talk to persuade me into joining his team. I should have begun to think that he had changed his mind about my potential, but for knowing him to be an old fox. Doubtless he had decided that a 'soft sell' would be more effective.

Anna and I spent one night together in London, then flew to Oslo. Before we left for Heathrow, a courier arrived from the Colonel, bringing me a bound folder that was about an inch thick.

'Something to read on the flight', said a paperclipped note. 'Keep it with you in the cabin'.

This meant do not place it in any item of luggage that is to be checked in. I kept the folder in my hand while we taxied and took off.

Anna, doubtless still tired after her flight from Moscow, leaned on my shoulder and was asleep within minutes.

I opened the folder and saw at once that I was right about the old fox. Between the covers was the soft sell *par excellence.*

Disguised as the manuscript of an aspiring novelist was a report of the more sensational activities of the Colonel's station, all attributed to one fictional and obviously superhuman spy. Clipped inside at the front were both a covering letter to a major publishing house and a reply, dated more than three months later, rejecting the story as being 'impossible to the point of absurdity'.

These precautions for the event of the manuscript's falling into the wrong hands were reinforced by an atrocious prose style that would surely weary the reader and make him cast the thing aside within the first couple of pages.

My initial reaction was to smile. As I read on, my respect for the Colonel deepened.

Even before we began our descent to Oslo, I had read sufficient about his covert operations to convince me that I should join the Twelvetrees team.

Intending us to see as much of Norway as was practical during our four weeks, I hired a car at Oslo airport and headed off inland.

At appropriate moments during our tour, I read further into the bogus novel. The Colonel had created a section specializing in 'dirty tricks' while fighting the Germans, and the Cold War had made it necessary to establish a permanent department. There were records of assassinations and abductions, sabotage, 'rustling' (i.e., capture of the other side's equipment), the spreading of misinformation, the 'turning' of enemy agents to work for us, the recruitment of agents at the very highest levels in foreign governments, the penetration of opposing intelligence services, and very much more.

By the time we visited the Vemork hydro-electric plant, I had read everything in the folder's pages. Vemork had been the scene of wartime sabotage efforts, and I was interested in seeing the site of these operations.

My plan had been to drive from there to the North Cape, returning via coastal roads. Anna vetoed this. 'No, Gregushka. It's too much driving for you. Let us find a quiet place where we can stay, go for walks and enjoy our surroundings. After a few days, if we feel like it, we can move on. But not every day moving on, for all of our four weeks'.

Of course she was right, and of course we did as she said. Thanks to her common sense, those four weeks became as near a replication of our honeymoon as could be imagined.

To allow Anna a short break before she was to fly back to Moscow, we returned to the UK two days earlier than was strictly necessary.

We went to see the Colonel together. 'You've found a publisher', I told him, handing back the weighty folder.

'And you have found your natural home', he responded.

Since then I have had many occasions to reflect on that remark. Doubtless it was accurate enough. Certainly I could not imagine myself doing anything else.

With Anna, things were entirely different. I had always opposed her being drawn into the Service. Not until years later did I find out what it was that she wanted. By then, it was too late.

X

The Colonel had not after all exaggerated when he promised that I should find the work at Twelvetrees both challenging and exciting.

His was the active arm of the intelligence service. The Colonel's unit was no more concerned with day-to-day running of our agents in other countries than it was with keeping an eye on foreign spies in our own. These routine but indispensable tasks were the province of the Service's major departments. At Twelvetrees we practised disruption. We were specialists, for instance, in turning the other side's agents.

There are few cases that it would be proper, or even legal, for me to disclose. I shall describe only two, where no more damage can be done. One of the more satisfying jobs concerned the headmistress of a school in Berkshire. This woman had been a devoted Communist since her early student days. GRU, Soviet military intelligence, recruited her while she was still undergoing teacher training, ordering her not to develop a public profile.

She carried out much of the organization of 'peace rallies', anti-nuclear protests and the like, while herself staying in the background.

On GRU orders, this woman struck up a friendship with a design engineer at the Hawker Siddeley aircraft company.

Once the association had ripened into intimacy, she confronted the engineer, a married man, with photographic proof of their relationship. For her silence, she demanded data on Hawker's work in developing a vertical take-off and landing (VTOL) aircraft.

The engineer was not intimidated by this threat to his marriage. He reported the approach to a security officer at his works. The case came to Twelvetrees.

We instructed the engineer to comply with his mistress's demands, but initially to plead some delay in his ability to obtain the data. Meanwhile, he was to bring selected documents to us.

With the engineer's aid, we doctored very slightly the data that he produced.

There was no surprise at our end when Soviet efforts to build VTOL aircraft met with endless problems and were ultimately abandoned. Hawker, as is well enough known, went on to produce its very successful Harrier.

We had filmed the headmistress's meetings with both the engineer and her GRU contact. Now we threatened her with lengthy imprisonment. This would mean separation for good from her little boy, to whom she was passionately attached. This boy, the product of an earlier love affair with a young architect, would be taken into care while she was on trial. Once she was committed to prison, he would be put out for adoption. She would never see him again.

Alternatively, the woman could work for us.

Understandably, she grasped this opportunity to keep both her liberty and her son. What was more, we paid her a little. For years thereafter this woman supplied us with invaluable details of GRU and KGB recruits in Britain, of Soviet involvement in the Northern Irish troubles and lists of what data Soviet intelligence was anxious to obtain.

We were happy to fulfil Soviet wishes, and Moscow's men were delighted to receive the misleading material with which we fed them.

The only mystery to us was how, in those days, the relevant education authority had come to appoint as a headmistress an unmarried woman with an illegitimate son.

This son is now one of the most famous faces and names in Britain. I am not going to say in which field.

In another operation, we violated, I regret to say, the neutrality of a friendly country. This was entirely my responsibility, and I have no hesitation in acknowledging my misbehaviour.

Years before, at the time of the Cuban missile confrontation, we had a man, Colonel Oleg Penkovsky, right at the heart of the Soviet General Staff. From Penkovsky we learned of the inaccuracy and limited range of Soviet missiles, as well as details of inadequate preparedness within Soviet forces. This inside information gave Western leaders the confidence to call Moscow's bluff.

Penkovsky did not come out of it so well. He was discovered and shot.

It seemed unlikely that we should find another source as well situated.

A prospect seemed to arise with a message from one of our agents in Austria, codename Cuckoo. This man, a fierce anti-Nazi, had begun working for Moscow during the war. Like many another formerly passionate Communist, Cuckoo changed his views during the post-war occupation of his country. When he offered his services to us, we asked him to continue in Moscow's pay. As a double agent, Cuckoo functioned magnificently for us. He was now the senior Soviet agent in Austria, as well as one of our best men overall.

Cuckoo became of sudden interest to Twelvetrees when his Soviet controller asked him to look for a small hotel that could be purchased in an area popular with tourists. A specific order was that the matter was to be kept secret from members of the Austrian Communist Party.

We told Cuckoo to go ahead but not to inform Moscow of a find until after he had alerted us.

Some four weeks later, a postcard arrived from Salzburg with the words 'Wish you were here'. This was Cuckoo's pre-arranged method of asking for a meeting in that city. The Colonel sent me.

I met Cuckoo at the Salzburg home of 'Uncle Fred', a former lawyer who had been struck off (and dealt a lengthy prison sentence) for having worked as a prosecutor at Gestapo headquarters. Uncle Fred was not one of our agents. As a dedicated anti-Communist, he merely provided us when necessary with a safe house.

What Cuckoo had to report was that he had found two likely hotels that were prospective purchases. The first was in Graz, the other in a rural setting at a junction on the road between Salzburg and Gmunden. A senior man from Moscow was expected shortly to inspect both. Moreover, being dissatisfied with recent results, this visitor wished to address Moscow's Austrian agents in an effort to stir them to further, and more fruitful, activity.

This did not ring true. A string of agents is not a team of salesmen. Senior men do not organize meetings like area managers, giving pep talks to increase results. Men in the field, who are better unknown to each other, are not gathered together in one place. Nor do top men expose themselves unnecessarily by ventures into hostile territory.

It looked to me like a trap, but with what object I could not imagine. I decided to counter with a trap of my own. A honey trap.

First, I asked for a half dozen men from Twelvetrees, knowing full well that six would not be available. I was right. Two arrived.

Cuckoo was to provide a voluptuous young lady.

Next I drove out with Cuckoo and my Twelvetrees reinforcements to check over the two premises that Cuckoo had found. First we stopped at the one located on a country road. The four of us went in for a drink and a discreet look round. A two-storey building, it had the advantage of standing alone and offering a clear field of fire in all directions. No other habitable buildings were within sight. A disadvantage from the point of view of escape was that there were only three roads leading away from the spot. All were easily blocked.

The hotel at Graz, though smaller, was more promising. Its location offered a great number of potential escape routes. Across the road were both a café and a bar.

Two days later, Cuckoo reported that his visitor from Moscow had named a rendezvous: Schönbrunn, Vienna, in forty eight hours' time.

I toyed with the idea of presenting one of my men as an agent in Cuckoo's team. This was impossible. Full details of everyone recruited had routinely to be sent through to Moscow Centre for approval. Neither of my men matched any of Cuckoo's agents in the slightest way. Nor could either speak German.

The man from Moscow, with two bodyguards, crossed the border out of Hungary in a car with Hungarian number plates. When he arrived at Schönbrunn to meet Cuckoo, I and my two men were already there. We photographed the newcomers and followed their car to Graz. Cuckoo took his visitor into the small hotel, leaving the two bodyguards in the car.

We took seats in the café opposite and sat where we could watch. An hour later, we were following the Russians on their way to the second hotel, out towards Salzburg.

Once I had seen the Russians turn in, I drove right on past, and stopped round a bend in the road. Ten minutes later, I watched from cover as one of the thugs emerged from the building to take two suitcases from the boot of the party's car.

We drove back to our own accommodation, developed the pictures we had taken and sent them via our embassy in Vienna to Twelvetrees, for the Russians to be identified.

Late that night I received a telephone call from Uncle Fred. Cuckoo was on his way.

I drove to Uncle Fred's alone. Cuckoo was already there. He showed me three hundred and fifty thousand US dollars that the Russian had given him as a down payment on the hotel in Graz. Cuckoo was to carry out the purchase. The Russian was not to be involved, except for supplying any extra currency required. He would be staying for two nights at the rural property, a move which ensured that he would not be remembered at Graz.

One by one in the course of the following day – Cuckoo was given an exact schedule – each of his agents was to report to the hotel to be examined by the Russian. Cuckoo was to be present throughout.

I used the next morning to reconnoitre the surroundings of the building and to find the best stations for my men.

Why the network wanted an hotel was clear. It was a place where a variety of people could call at irregular hours without arousing suspicion. Run by one of their own, it would be the ultimate safe house, ideal as a courier drop as well as a photographic workshop, a centre for cryptology, preliminary analysis of data and a dozen other activities.

Surely, though, the Austrian network – no more than eleven agents including Cuckoo – could scarcely justify such an expenditure of hard-won foreign currency. It seemed to me that once in Moscow's hands the hotel would be used to serve all Western European networks.

There would be legitimate visitors, too, providing a small income to offset running costs. Austria was a regular destination for French, Italian, Dutch, West German and even Spanish tourists.

Cuckoo's agents were to be examined by his controller in a search for a couple able to run the hotel – ideally, a man to manage and do deciphering and photographic work, a woman to attend to the kitchen and other matters. Two men might also prove suitable.

From concealed positions, my two men and I kept observation on the hotel next day. We photographed every one of Cuckoo's agents, both arriving and leaving. All were known to us.

Cuckoo left in the early evening. We returned to our own rooms, where a response from headquarters arrived via our embassy. Cuckoo's controller had been identified as one of Moscow's top men, a veteran network handler known on our side as Dolores.

Our orders were to report all his movements and contacts to headquarters. A man from Russia Section would be arriving next day to take over.

I met Cuckoo later. He confirmed that after the purchase at Graz had been completed, two agents of long standing were to move in. Dolores and his bodyguards would be leaving tomorrow morning.

I told Cuckoo to forget the voluptuous young lady, prepare to leave, keep the three hundred and fifty thousand dollars on his person and stand by the telephone.

Next morning, my two men and I were outside the rural hotel shortly before daybreak. I had a man in a concealed position on a grassy slope on either side of the building. Each was armed.

I myself, unarmed, sat in our car parked in a shallow layby out of sight on the Gmunden side of the building. We were in communication by walkie-talkie.

I had a view through tall grass of the hotel's front door. When one of Dolores's bodyguards emerged to replace suitcases in the boot, I started my engine and put the others on to instant alert. They should now be just behind each front corner of the hotel, weapons in hand.

Dolores ambled out of the front door, drew in a deep breath, then paused to light a cigarette. He was a man only just in his fifties, stocky and of medium height. Such hair as he had was grey and cropped. The bodyguards were standing either side of him, looking along the road in each direction. Dolores was on his way back behind the Iron Curtain, and there was no time to wait for any Johnny-come-lately from Russia Section.

I let in my clutch and shot the car forward towards the hotel. At the same instant I saw my men launch themselves round the corners of the building and towards Dolores's bodyguards.

One succeeded in hurling his man to the ground and disarming him. My second man, fired on before he could reach his target, was obliged to return a bullet. The bodyguard dropped.

By that time I was on the scene. I leaped out of the car to help bundle Dolores into the back seat. My men were quicker. One had already knocked him out.

I turned to drop into the driving seat. Before I was quite there, I felt a searing blow in my lower back and was punched forward as though kicked by a horse. Only the open door stopped my sprawling on to my face. The odd thing is that I do not remember hearing the shot.

I fell inside, banged the car back into gear and rocketed away along the road towards Salzburg.

Dolores was no trouble. Not with a man jammed in on either side of him and a hypodermic syringe thrust into his arm.

This was scarcely a textbook operation. Pleased as I was with the result, I could not be proud of its execution.

We should at the least have disabled the opposition's car, but failed to do so. As a result, I was forced to take evasive action in case Dolores's goons were following. I turned off the main road at the first opportunity and took a roundabout route towards the border with West Germany.

Better still, we should have taken the car. That would not only have eliminated the possibility of pursuit, but given us Dolores's suitcases. These might have yielded interesting contents.

Ideally, we should also have made sure of disarming the second bodyguard, the one who was wounded but had proved himself still capable of firing. This, however, might have cost us one of our men.

These omissions were entirely my fault. I had leaped into action without thinking all possibilities through. All in all, it had been a pretty crude operation.

The other side had made omissions, too, not that these in any way excused my own. Why did Dolores not have a second car with goons looking out for his back? I had scouted around and seen no one at all in the vicinity of the hotel.

Once we felt clear of any pursuit, we stopped at a lakeside for my back to be examined. The bullet had entered the pelvis to the right of the spine. It had not come out. There was little bleeding. My back would stiffen up later, that was certain, but all that mattered at the time was crossing into Germany. Once we had left Austria behind, with no one on our tail, I could relax. A Hungarian car would not pass through the border without difficulties.

Dolores was bulkier than he looked. We pushed him onto the floor and covered him with a dark blanket. My two men rested their feet on him.

Along the way, we telephoned Cuckoo and told him to make his way by rail and cross-channel ferry to London. He was experienced enough, I knew, to conceal the dollars successfully.

Ten minutes later, we were in Germany. I moved into the front passenger seat, stretched out my legs and let one of the others drive.

Here, in Bavaria, was the American zone. I was reluctant to draw in our allies to a potential diplomatic crisis, and determined to wait until we reached the British zone in the north before seeking treatment.

As we progressed, I became light-headed, and soon fell asleep (some say that I fainted; they may well be right). I did not wake until we turned into the BAOR hospital at Rinteln.

The bullet was removed, leaving me, so I am told (I have never been able to see it), with a neat L-shaped scar below my waist. Dolores was treated, too, in the form of long-term sedation. The RAF gave us a lift home to Northolt, where a trio from Twelvetrees was waiting for us.

The Colonel was delighted with our prize. After I completed a full report, he sent me on sick leave. I declined his offer to arrange home leave for Anna.

'I don't want her to see me like this', I told him. The fact was that I had been ordered into hospital to allow severed muscles and nerves a chance to heal.

'This doesn't count as your sick leave', said the Colonel. 'Undergoing hospital treatment for wounds received in the field is part of your duties. Stick with it until you really are as fit as you have ever been. *Then* you can go on sick leave, once you're in a position to enjoy it'.

I had a strong suspicion that the Colonel had made this up, but did not challenge him.

Never had I known the man in such liberal humour. He was right, though. It was wise to take advantage of the rest that was offered, or I might not have finished in the more or less intact state that I did regain.

Thanks to severed muscles, I still limp occasionally, badly enough to earn me a blue disabled parking badge, Naturally, I regard such a trivial wound as a minimal price to have paid for the pleasure of handing over Dolores to our inquisitors.

To universal surprise, there were no repercussions. All were braced for diplomatic protests from the Austrian government, but none came. The most surprising thing was that, despite three shots having been fired outside their front door, the hotel people seemed to have noticed nothing. No incident was reported.

Dolores's two bodyguards had, it seemed, disappeared with their car.

On our side, we set up Cuckoo with a new identity, paid for chiefly with Moscow's dollars. For all our determined efforts over the next years, Dolores steadfastly refused to be 'turned'. Again, this was my fault. I had abducted the man without first having trapped him into something that we could use as a lever against him.

XI

From the day that the Colonel rescued me from that business at headquarters, I had been growing steadily closer to him. His efforts to keep Anna from me were long forgiven, and forgotten. We now shared a common distaste for what we both saw as the by-the-book plodders at the head of the Service. For their part, these gentlemen saw everyone at Twelvetrees as mavericks, even roughnecks. They certainly did not like me. I had the impression that they resented the very existence of any special unit outwith their direct day-to-day control. *De jure* of course, the Colonel and Twelvetrees were very much subordinate to headquarters. *De facto*, the Colonel behaved as though answerable to no one. It seemed to me that the Colonel fabricated rules as he went along. That whole business of trying to keep Anna and me apart – that wasn't headquarters' doing; it was his. I was astonished one day to hear him quote a one-time Commander-in-Chief of the German Army, whose favourite saying was apparently 'Regulations are for the stupid ones'.

'That surprises you, Greig, doesn't it?' he asked. 'The last thing you would expect to hear from a German, perhaps, but if you think about it, it makes sense. The Germans encouraged individual initiative, and that's what made them such blighters to fight'.

I was not privy to the discussions that the Colonel had with the chief of the Service, but find no difficulty in picturing the acrimony expressed on both sides. Whenever the Colonel was summoned to Headquarters, he first tried to avoid or delay the meeting. By the time that finally he went, he would be wound up well into fighting mood. On his return, he was invariably more red-faced than usual yet always cheerily disposed. Whether he had won his argument or been forced to concede, we could not read in his manner. The joy that he took in battle, irrespective of outcome, was always apparent in his glittering eyes. After a lively clash the man was pepped up into joviality for the rest of the day.

When I returned to the UK with Dolores, I was summoned to headquarters along with the Colonel. I was expected to explain myself to a leadership that was far from amused. Devotees of the fictional spy story will be sceptical of official assurances that the Service issues to its agents neither licences to kill nor double-0 numbers. As you see, none of us is a superman. We make mistakes, and are all subject to the ordinary pains of our loves, our work and our home lives. Most people will probably assume that such disavowals are lies. We all prefer the sensational story, and are likely to feel heartily indignant towards anyone who would, for example, prove to us beyond any doubt that there *is* no monster in Loch Ness. Such being the natural inclinations of human nature, few will want to believe that officially the Service not only frowns on killing, but also renounces abduction.

Any idea stirring inside me that on bringing in Dolores I should receive congratulations from headquarters was smothered at birth. I was, apparently, a blackguard. The Colonel was overjoyed, headquarters angry. We were expected, it appeared, to stick to Marquis of Queensbury rules against an opponent slashing at us with a cutlass. The chief seemed to have forgotten the time when abductions had been practically everyday routine for the other side. A favourite trick of the Communists in Berlin had been to send in heavies against a target on a street in the West. Running away from his would-be abductors, the quarry would – heaven-sent blessing! – discover a taxi just within reach. Breathing silent thanks, the prey would leap into the safety of the car, to find, once inside, that the doors mysteriously locked and that the journey ended in East Berlin. For once I – no, not I alone; it took three of us to pull it off – had reversed this train of seizures. The Communists' fake taxi resulted, of course, from planning and preparation. I had simply seen an opportunity and taken it. For such mischief, I was to be hauled over the coals. In particular, it appeared that the gentlemen of Russia Section were greatly displeased at my poaching in what they, no doubt naturally, considered their own exclusive waters. Sending me at once on sick leave was the Colonel's way of circumventing my carpeting. He himself was called to answer for my conduct and so, of course, were my two unfortunate subordinates. This was unjust in that the responsibility was mine alone. I had made the decision to capture Dolores. The colonel knew nothing of my intention and had been presented with a *fait accompli*. The other two had acted on my instructions, and might well be presumed to have supposed that I too was acting under orders. In such a case, they would assume the action to have been legitimate. No blame could attach to them.

In my hospital bed I wrote a full report detailing these facts and admitting sole responsibility. Naturally, this was not considered good enough. Headquarters sent a pompous individual to my bedside with a tape recorder and a list of loaded questions. I treated him politely and pleaded guilty to all implied transgressions. The rocket I received from the chief was as lurid as he could make it. Did I think that life in the Service was an anthology of Boys' Own Adventure Stories? Did I not realize that by engaging in irresponsible, unauthorized conduct of this kind I was encouraging the other side to retaliation, thus jeopardizing our own men and women in the field? Furthermore, I had disobeyed a direct order, which had been to await the arrival of a senior man from Russia Section. Any such disobedience in future would have the gravest possible consequences for my future, and so on and so on.

Some of this criticism was certainly justified. None of our agents suffered in retaliation, though, since Moscow did not know who it was that had carried out the abduction. The official reaction to what I considered a useful act of initiative on my part sealed an almost conspiratorial alliance between the Colonel and myself. If it had not been for that imperiousness of his that had inspired Anna to christen him 'his majesty', I should be tempted to say that from then on we both behaved a little like the proverbial naughty schoolboys.

Certainly my Austrian adventure seemed to have drawn the two of us into a warm intimacy which I had previously been unable to imagine. The Colonel visited me several times while I was in hospital. On the day before I was discharged he came again and placed a bottle of sixteen years old single malt whisky on the bedside table. He had never before called me by my Christian name. He did so now.

'Ian, you know that I am approaching retirement age'.

I had never thought about it.

'Three years to go, unless they want to get rid of me earlier'.

They would certainly try. I was sure of that.

'Someone will have to take over'.

Unless they close down the place altogether. That seemed to me more likely.

'Do you know how old I was when I took charge?'

'No idea, Colonel'.

'I was ten years younger than you are now'.

Of course. It was wartime, and things happened fast then.

'Ian, some years ago I had a young man with every attribute necessary to run Twelvetrees after I had gone. He looked the ideal successor. I took him under my wing and was preparing him to be my deputy. Then he was killed on a silly job'. The Colonel looked at me hard. 'Since I say that it was a silly job, no doubt you can guess where it happened'.

'It must have been the Balkans'.

'Bang right, Ian. I tell you, it was a job that any one of a dozen others could have done. I've never forgiven myself since for letting him go there. You know what Frederick the Great said?'

'That the whole of the Balkans were not worth the life of one Prussian grenadier'.

'Exactly. I should have remembered that before I foolishly let my best man go to his death'. The Colonel brought down the flat of his hand on his knee, drew up his shoulders and looked squarely at me. 'Well, it's too late to do anything about that now. The thing is, Ian, it's because, alongside your specific talents, you have the right instincts, that I want you to come back from your sick leave fighting fit and ready to start learning to become my successor. I'll get you an upgrade in status if I can, and in any case have you named officially as my deputy. I'll see to that'.

XII

Eventually, the upgrade in status came through, and I could not help wondering what battles the Colonel had needed to fight before he could secure it for me. The upgrade meant a little more money, but welcome as this was, it was not the important thing.

What mattered were the impending responsibilities towards which I was heading. It was typical of the Colonel that he had not asked me whether I wished to be his successor. My acquiescence was taken for granted, and he simply issued an order.

In truth, I was far from convinced that I had the qualities necessary to run an entire department. The Dolores affair had shot me up in the Colonel's estimation, and that made me a little uncomfortable. After all, I had done no more than drive, and even that for only a minor distance. It was our two goons who had disabled Dolores's bodyguards and overpowered the man himself.

I had never really proved myself in the field, whereas there were plenty who had. I could run a string of agents without trouble, and thought that I could interrogate satisfactorily enough. I could claim no more.

It seemed to me that there was a natural tendency to promote people into positions that demanded more from them than they could supply. They would then fall flat on their faces. To know one's own limitations was, I had long felt, a basic requirement of adulthood. So many disasters originated in someone's overestimate of his own capabilities. Look at Hitler.

I had no wish to take on more than I could carry out with competence. What was more, I still preferred the chance of more action to any form of deskwork. I knew of course that excursions into the field would have to end some day, but was in no hurry for that day to arrive.

The Colonel was right about one thing. Headquarters did push him into retirement earlier than was strictly necessary. A whole year earlier. I feared then that the opportunity would be taken to close down Twelvetrees, and was surprised both that it survived and that I was kept on as its head.

Even the deadest of dead heads at Headquarters could not avoid acknowledging the occasional need for a dirty tricks department. I felt sure, too, that they preferred any such institution to be somewhere well away from themselves, a department that they could disown if our political masters turned nasty.

At the first sign of any embarrassment, the Pontius Pilates at Headquarters would be falling over themselves to wash their hands of any responsibility. I was there to carry the can and to be thrown to the wolves when necessary.

Twelvetrees was not only useful. It was essential, not just because of the work it carried out but because no government organization can function without a subordinate division on hand to take any blame.

I bought a house near Twelvetrees, where Anna and I could live until my retirement. That, I promised myself, would not be too late in life. Retirement years, when they came, would be spent in Scotland.

Meanwhile, I had a pond constructed outside our lounge window, from where one could hear rain pattering on lily pads. This was no more than a running joke between us, and it was really my only contribution to the place. I left to Anna the remainder of the garden layout, along with furnishing and decoration inside the house. I knew that she would plan and carry out these works with a woman's innate good sense. I, on the other hand, was likely to overcrowd rooms or introduce clashes of design and colour.

Anna was delighted to undertake these responsibilities. After she had devoted her next leave to them, we had a remarkably cosy home and the beginnings of a garden that promised colour all year round.

Anna stayed on at our embassy in Moscow, taking home leave usually twice a year. When she was at home we listened together to a great deal of music. Rachmaninov was high on our list of favourites, as was in particular the first violin concerto by Max Bruch. 'Play it for me, Gregushka', Anna would say, and I knew which recording to put on.

When I brought Dolores to Britain I had promised myself a sizeable gain in inside information from Soviet intelligence. It did not work out as well as I hoped. Not only did I fail to turn Dolores, but he told us little. What was more, headquarters repeatedly pointed out that hanging on to him was proving an expensive business.

I visited Dolores several times at the institution where he was detained. I could not expect him to receive me amiably, but he surprised me by being far less resentful than I had any right to suppose. No, he had no complaints about his accommodation as far as it went, and overall the food met with his approval. I asked about his wishes for tobacco and alcohol, and was able to satisfy these. Beyond a 'Thank you' he made no comment, but I could see that he was taken aback at such treatment. Let him tell them that when he goes back home, I said to myself. We had a sizeable library of books in Russian, and I was able to take him, or send to him, every title for which he asked. In time we became, I felt, quite chummy in a coolly official way.

We never did recruit another man as highly placed as Penkovsky. The Service was disappointed, but as the years passed the lack of top class intelligence was felt less acutely. Relations with Moscow were thawing noticeably.

The freeze came back after Brezhnev's death. His successor, Yuri Andropov, had been the longest serving head of the KGB. Andropov was notorious for his suppression of dissidents and for having crushed the 'Prague spring'.

He did not last long. Andropov died only fifteen months after Brezhnev. He was succeeded by Konstantin Tchernenko, whose term of office, as far as I was concerned, was marked chiefly by the arrest of Anna.

The Foreign Office made what representations it could, citing Anna's diplomatic immunity. Moscow rejected all appeals with the argument that her conduct had rendered such immunity null and void.

This was a curious, perhaps even unique, justification. The usual procedure when diplomatic immunity is deemed to have been violated is of course to revoke it and expel the offender.

As to what Anna's alleged misconduct had been, Moscow maintained an icy wall of silence.

Our Service enjoyed good sources of what we called 'social intelligence'. It was astonishing what crumbs of seemingly unconnected material could be picked up at parties, receptions, dinners and even social evenings dedicated to games of cards. Fitted together correctly, such grains of information could often produce an unsuspected and significant picture. So far, this was the sort of intelligence that Anna had delivered. The Colonel, so he told me later, was reluctant to assign Anna to higher grade tasks, and had repeatedly put off the day when he would ask her to do more.

Now Anna was herself the subject of this so-called 'social intelligence'. We asked for, and received, an apparently comprehensive picture from several of our Moscow sources. These confirmed that Anna had been popular throughout the leading strata of Soviet society and a regular guest at diplomatic and ministerial receptions. She had enjoyed the confidence of men at the very top,

116

and was trusted to an extent almost unknown among foreigners. Her arrest came as a shock to all. Everyone who knew her found it inexplicable.

If those on the spot found Anna's arrest baffling, what chance had I of understanding it, seated fifteen hundred miles away behind the great oak desk that I had inherited from the Colonel?

My own theory was that Moscow had discovered who was behind the abduction of Dolores. This was Moscow's retaliation, aimed at me personally.

When we seized Dolores, I believed that the Russians would suspect either West Germany or the Americans. The Colonel had concurred with this view.

Now I had to accept that meantime something had convinced them of my part in the affair. It seemed that they had definite information pointing to me, or at least to the British Service. It was an open question whether they would have taken such decisive action if they had no more than suspicion.

My first thought was to offer myself as Moscow's prisoner in exchange for Anna. Almost immediately I realized that I could not do this. I should be unable to guarantee resistance to Soviet interrogation methods, and was certain to betray far too many people. Here was a situation where it was undeniably essential not to overestimate one's own strengths and abilities.

There was little for it but to rely on the efforts of the Foreign Office, and to be patient.

We had a man inside Butyrka Prison in Moscow. Communication was always subject to a certain delay, and it was almost three months before we had his confirmation that no one answering Anna's description had been among recent admissions.

It was in any case more likely that Anna had been taken to KGB headquarters at the Lubyanka. Of the great yellow-bricked

Lubyanka it was said that it offered the most distant view in Moscow, that even from its cellars one could see Siberia. Reports from the Lubyanka were intermittent and usually lagged months behind events. In time we received news of a woman, described as 'most beautiful' and a 'foreigner', whose presence there was creating quite a stir among Lubyanka personnel.

I thought that I should go mad with worry. Concentration on my work was suffering, as it had done all those years before, when I had met Anna only once and was trying to shake off my obsession with her. I began contemplating two ideas: Resignation or asking the Colonel to return while I took a back seat.

I had already telephoned the Colonel to ask if I could drive over to Cheltenham to see him, when news arrived that Tchernenko too had died. He had lasted in office for an even shorter period than his predecessor.

'Hang on, my boy' was the Colonel's advice. 'A lot may change now'.

Certainly much did change. Reforms introduced by the next Soviet leader, Mikhail Gorbachev, were misinterpreted in the West as 'liberalization'. They encouraged the Foreign Office to revive its efforts on Anna's behalf. In vain.

Gorbachev's reforms were intended to make Communism stronger. Their effect was the opposite. Gorbachev brought about the collapse of the Soviet Union.

I was completely taken aback by the speed with which this happened. I had always believed that if the West remained strong enough and never slackened its pace, Communism would ultimately be driven into breakdown. I had not, though, expected this to happen before another thirty years or so.

Now Gorbachev was replaced by Boris Yeltsin, head of the new (non-Communist) Russian Federation. This total change of régime finally created a more relaxed atmosphere, putting the Foreign

Office into a position to negotiate an exchange of prisoners. Dolores and several others were to be flown back to Moscow, Anna returned to Britain.

I wanted to go to Moscow to accompany Anna on the machine that would bring her to London, but the Russians would not permit this. Despite the improvement in relations, I was still *persona non grata* for the Kremlin.

Instead, I was at Heathrow to see Dolores and some others board the unscheduled Russian flight that was due to take off at the same time that Anna's machine departed from Moscow. On either side I was flanked by a group of men, each standing apart from the other like opposing families at a wedding. All that was missing, I thought, was a master of ceremonies announcing: 'In the blue corner, Foreign Office officials. In the red, men from the Russian Embassy'.

Not until the gangway into the Tupolev was in position did our goons bring out Dolores and the others who were to be repatriated.

Before beginning to mount into the aircraft, Dolores paid me the distinction of a lengthy scowl. This, I was sure, was chiefly for the benefit of the watching delegation from his embassy. I tried hard to remain expressionless.

The two families, still strangers to one another, did not disperse until the machine had lifted and was turning onto its flight path. From our own embassy in Moscow we had confirmation meanwhile that Anna too was in the air.

XIII

The flight time from Moscow was put at three and a half hours. I was too excited to wait either at Heathrow, at home or in my office. I found a minor road as quickly as I could, and spent the time driving through the countryside away from the airport, pottering slowly through village after village along roads that were mostly unknown to me.

It was inevitable that I should find myself looking at the dashboard clock every five minutes or so. It took all the discipline that I could summon to prevent myself arriving back at the airport an hour before Anna's machine landed.

In the end, I was there twenty minutes before her flight was due.

Foreign Office people were there, too. That annoyed me. Did they have to be on the spot? Our reunion was a private occasion that needed no onlookers.

I saw Anna's aircraft land, and watched it disappear towards the far end of the runway. By the time that it had turned and was taxiing back, I was almost in a fever. With as much decorum as I could summon, I walked along so as to be opposite the aircraft doors when they opened. In my hand was a bouquet of the flowers I knew to be Anna's favourites.

The aircraft came to a halt, its engines rose briefly to a final whistle and stopped. To my right, two men in white coats, accompanied by a nurse, were wheeling a hospital-style trolley out onto the tarmac.

I knew before the cabin door opened that it would be Anna who was carried down from the machine.

All other passengers descended before the men in white coats went up for the stretcher. A BEA stewardess carried down Anna's bag.

I was at the trolley before they lifted Anna on to it.

'Gregushka'. The voice, and the voice alone, was the same. On the face there was not enough flesh now for dimples. The eyes that had twinkled and enchanted were dulled, all sparkle gone. Hair once curled, coiling and lustrous hung limp without sheen.

I bent over to hold and kiss the woman I loved. My God! She was all bone.

'I'm all right, Gregushka', she said. 'Just tired'.

I walked alongside the trolley holding Anna's hand, while they wheeled her inside. An airport doctor took Anna's pulse, listened to her chest, measured her blood pressure.

He stood upright and turned to me. 'If I say debilitated', he said, 'I mean that this is the worst case of sheer debilitation that I have ever seen. She needs to be built back up quickly'.

I could see that for myself. 'Is there…' I asked, 'Is there…'

'You mean, is there anything seriously or fundamentally wrong?'

I could only nod.

'I can see nothing, but that doesn't mean a thing. She needs a comprehensive examination. Take her home, have her examined by your own doctor and build her up'.

I thanked the man and went with Anna in the ambulance to our home. A nurse accompanied us and supervised while two paramedics carried Anna in to our bed.

Tomorrow I should send someone to fetch my car from Heathrow. And tomorrow, I knew, I should submit my resignation from the Service. Anna was my occupation from now on. She was my profession, my calling and my life.

My terms of service did not allow me to bow out without lengthy notice, but I knew that compassionate leave would cover this.

122

Even so, there were still some matters from which I could not walk away. I needed to hand over the running of the department to my deputy, a duty which would involve attendance at Twelvetrees probably for at least two weeks.

Most important, though, was Anna's debriefing. It would not be appropriate for her husband to carry this out, and strictly speaking it was a task for Russia Section. In view of Anna's frailty, though, I was doubtful that she would cooperate fully with a stranger. The solution was to ask the Colonel to step temporarily out of retirement. He knew Anna better than anyone, perhaps in some ways even better than I did.

The Colonel had kept in touch with me throughout Anna's imprisonment. He had several times offered to lend his weight to negotiations for an exchange – something that the Foreign Office seemed to feel would be more of a hindrance than a help.

To me, it seemed that the deal had come about in the end only thanks to the Russians' pride in always recovering their men.

I should have invited the Colonel to be at Heathrow when Anna landed, had it not been that I had anticipated an intimate reunion of a romantic nature. Now I felt some anger that our Moscow embassy had not seen fit to advise us of Anna's condition.

I telephoned the Colonel to put him in the picture and to ask if he would come and stay with us to debrief Anna, while I attended to handing-over matters at Twelvetrees.

If the man could have dived through the telephone wire and appeared at my side instantly, I am sure that he would have done so.

He was there that evening. When he saw Anna, I swear that tears flooded his eyes. And this was the man of whom Anna had said that he had no blood in him.

It was noticeable that he did not stay with Anna long, but fairly rushed from the room to use a handkerchief. As he stuffed the linen back into his pocket, he began to curse everyone in the KGB, the GRU, the Russian government, the Russian Foreign Ministry, the Russian police, the Russian forces, the Communist Party – practically everyone in Russia save for the Bolshoi Ballet. That day I learned words that I had never heard before.

Alexander, alerted by the Colonel, arrived next morning. So did our doctor.

Alexander turned white when he saw his sister.

The doctor spent very nearly an hour checking Anna thoroughly, pursed his lips, tut-tutted, came close to shaking his head and promised to arrange an early hospital examination.

Meanwhile I engaged a nurse to live in.

'I'm going to have to take this steadily, Ian', said the Colonel, once he had cooled down and gathered his thoughts as well as his feelings under control. 'I simply can't rush into questioning the poor girl. My God! Can you imagine what Russia Section would do to her if they got their hands on her?'

I could indeed, only too well. They would get the correct story out of Anna, yes, would find out everything that we needed to know, just as the Colonel would. But they would exhaust Anna in the process, hinder her recovery.

It needed a sympathetic someone to talk with her, to have a conversation, not conduct an interrogation.

Anna spent the next three days in hospital for a complete examination. While she was there, I fitted out a bedroom for her on the ground floor.

For eight days after that, while I was at Twelvetrees, and whenever the nurse was not ministering to her, the Colonel sat by Anna's bed with his tape recorder operating out of sight.

As our information indicated, she had been held the entire time in the Lubyanka. This was the first fact that emerged, and it took the Colonel half a day to get that far. It was also, for quite a time, the only fact that Anna would disclose.

'It's no good, Ian', the Colonel admitted. 'I'm sorry. I simply can't persuade her to talk about her time in the Lubyanka. Her mind just closes up when she sees that I am broaching the topic. It obviously hurts her, and I simply can't bear to do it'.

Was this the Colonel we had both known? The unrelenting autocrat dubbed 'his majesty'?

He persisted for a week, then came to me with tears on the point of spilling from his eyes. The distress in his voice was painful to hear. 'I really can't question her any more. It makes me feel like the most appalling brute. That poor, poor girl! Perhaps you are the only one she will ever talk to, if she even does that'.

Both the Foreign Office and the Service were waiting for reports. They would just have to be given all that there was: Anna had been kept the entire time in the Lubyanka and was unable to give any further details.

The Colonel was alarmed. 'You know what they'll do, don't you, Ian?'

'I know what they'll try to do. But it'll be over my dead body – and I mean that literally'.

The Service could send some clever devil to inject Anna with scopolamine or some other truth drug. Then he would run through a complete rota of pitiless questions.

They might not go this far, but in an extreme case it was not unthinkable.

I wasn't having that, and really would defend Anna from it with my life.

Results from Anna's hospital examination arrived on the morning that the Colonel was preparing to return to Cheltenham.

She was HIV positive.

I admit that I all but fainted. The blow hit me ten times harder than the bullet in my back had done.

I could see the shock on the Colonel's face as I practically fell into a chair. He brought me a whisky in double quick time and kept his arm round my shoulder while I drank.

'My dear chap, you've gone as white as a sheet of paper'.

Only seconds later, the Colonel too had folded onto a seat. His hand was steady, but only just, as he poured a dram for himself.

I sat some moments frozen in silence and horror before becoming aware of subdued muttering. The Colonel was again working his way, quietly this time, through his litany of curses.

XIV

The first thing I had to do was relieve the nurse of her duties. I sent her straight to the hospital for tests to ensure that Anna had passed on nothing to her.

Those were still relatively early days of dealing with HIV sufferers, and we certainly did not know it all. So much was then *terra nova,* even for the specialists.

What I knew was that from now on, apart of course from her doctor, I must be the only one to have close contact with Anna.

My mother expected the two of us to arrive in Argyll for a visit. She was upset when I explained that Anna was too ill to travel. 'Perhaps I should come down to give you a hand running the house', she suggested.

'Mother', I reasoned, 'I have been running it alone all the while that Anna has been away. Why should I need any help now that she is home?'

At all costs I must prevent my mother appearing. Were she to arrive, I knew that I should have considerable difficulty not only in explaining the facts but also in restraining her from injudicious embraces and displays of affection towards Anna. The last thing I wanted was to lose both my wife and my mother to AIDS.

Besides his visits to Anna, our doctor was notably helpful in checking myself regularly as well as keeping me abreast of the latest advances in knowledge of the condition.

It was three or four weeks after Anna's return before I realized that what I was trying to do, what the airport doctor had told me to do, was simply not working. I was trying desperately to build Anna up, and she was growing no stronger.

At first she ate slowly, but as the days passed sat up and tucked in with evident enjoyment. Even so, she put on no obvious flesh. Once she was able to stand, I began checking her weight daily. Progress was as good as non-existent. I installed a second CD player in Anna's bedroom and sat with her for hours while we listened together to favourite works.

Out of the blue one morning, she pleaded: 'Gregushka, I don't want to lie here for ever. Let me sit with you'.

Rejoicing at this amount of progress, I helped Anna out of bed and through to the lounge. Once I had her settled in our most comfortable chair, I set the dining table for us both. After we had eaten and I had filled the dishwasher, I placed some Rachmaninov on the lounge player and set the volume low.

I sat down on the sofa, expecting Anna to settle beside me. Instead, she went onto her knees on the floor, burying her head into my lap and clasping my legs as though she were about to fall and they were the mainstays that would save her. I began stroking her hair, and soon became aware that she was sobbing without sound. I had never seen Anna other than strong in spirit and practically bursting with self-confidence. This emotional collapse was frightening.

'Oh, Gregushka' was all that she managed to say.

It seemed that Anna would stay that way for hours. Finally, though, I lifted her onto a sofa and gave her a handkerchief for her tears. 'You don't need to say anything, darling', I assured her. 'It is enough that you are here'. I took her face between my hands and looked into eyes that once had danced and were now frighteningly still and sunken. I kissed her forehead. 'Until I met you', I told her, 'I never knew that such exquisite happiness could exist'.

'Oh Gregushka, you'll start me off again'.

'Well we can't have that. How about a sherry?'

To my immense gratification, Anna not only nodded but managed a thin smile. I had an idea that sherry would be a good part of the building up process. We had each had one before our meal, and another now would, I was sure, do no harm.

That was the first step along Anna's hard road. Little by little from then on, she set about returning to as near a normal routine as was within the limits of her strength. She began to walk about the house, to sit in the garden, and to go out with me in the car. Before accompanying me in the two-seater for the first time, she sat down in front of her dressing table mirror and smiled a woeful smile. 'Don't I look a fright?'

'Of course you don't, darling'.

'Of course I do, and I'll show you just what I'm going to do about it'.

It really was like magic. Despite the most nourishing diet that the experts could recommend, Anna's face had remained gaunt. Yet in some miraculous fashion Anna found a combination of cosmetics that made it impossible for her to appear in any way emaciated. Instead, she looked simply beautiful. She had always been that, but now it was a different, a slimmer face that enchanted one.

I suppose women have all kinds of preparations for these things, because somehow Anna even managed to restore the sheen to her hair. What Anna had been through, goodness only knew. Whatever it was, it had ravaged her body to a pitiful degree. Yet now before my eyes I could see her spirit coming back to life.

During this period, Alexander visited again. He was so far pleased with Anna's evident progress that he invited the two of us out in his car.

Alexander took us to a restaurant where conversation with Anna, though hesitant, produced in her several smiles. She said nothing of her experiences to Alexander, but spoke of these only when she and I were back home.

Bit by bit, Anna began to talk, to give me, without my ever putting a single question, those answers that I needed, the answers for which the Colonel hoped, that headquarters demanded and the Foreign Office expected. I have kept them to myself until now.

The whole story did not emerge for more than a year. Without any prompting, Anna would reveal one small piece of her history. Then she would fall silent on the subject for perhaps a week.

There was no point in my trying to hurry her. I felt that she wanted me to know everything, but that the emotional stress of recalling her most horrific moments was too much for her to face. I reasoned that when she wanted me to know something more, she would tell me, but could do so only when she felt able to bear the pain of bringing past agonies to life. She could do this only in brief spurts, and when she could tolerate no more would relapse into silence or switch abruptly to a more cheerful subject.

In time, I became able to detect when Anna was reaching the point at which the hurt of remembrance was becoming too great. Then I would deflect her feelings by changing the topic. She would always smile and take up the fresh theme as though she had been waiting just for this.

XV

On a May morning that was particularly inviting, I took Anna out in the car for a drive along country lanes. Anna so much enjoyed the countryside with all its varied greens.

'Gregushka, England is so gentle', she had often exclaimed.

We stopped for lunch at the same restaurant where she had first heard rain plashing on lily pads. There was no rain today, nor even a hint of it; only the softest of spring sunlight with its promise of awakening life.

'Gregushka', Anna asked, 'do you remember the rain that first time?'

Could I ever forget?

Anna took my hand. 'And you were such a dear, creating lily ponds for me so that I could hear it again and again. On a roof, even'.

I clasped her hands in both of mine and raised them to my lips. 'That was just the very smallest expression of my love', I told her. 'For you I would do anything and everything. You know that, darling'.

We drove home slowly, drinking in the colours in the hedgerows and on the fields. Everywhere was the pledge of freshness.

Even onto the simple brickwork of our modest house the late afternoon sun painted an unambiguous and gilded welcome.

I stopped the car in our drive and went round to the passenger side, as I always did, to open the door for Anna and to help her with her seat belt.

'Gregushka!' There was alarm in her voice. 'I can't get up'.

I opened the house door first, then slid one arm under Anna's knees and the other round her shoulders. To lift her was so easy. She seemed to weigh almost nothing.

I carried Anna straight to her bedroom, helped to remove her outer clothes, softened her pillows and tucked her in.

Sunlight falling through the window lent a golden tone to her every feature. I stroked her hair, her cheek, lifted her hand, kissed it over and over.

'Gregushka', she whispered, 'you have been so good to me'.

I found it difficult to speak. Some blockage seemed to have appeared in my throat. 'It is you, darling', I told her, 'who have been unbelievably good to me'.

I managed to get out the words after a fashion, but don't know if I was articulate enough for her to hear. 'Every day I am still amazed at my incredible fortune. I know that I was never good enough for you to marry, yet …'

I tried to say more, but my speech box seemed to have dried up.

I leaned forward, kissed Anna's cheek, her forehead.

Two arms, wasted now as I had never seen them, twined themselves round my neck. For some minutes we were silent.

Anna was first to speak. Her voice, until now unchanged, had weakened like the rest of her.

'Will you play it for me, Gregushka, please?'

I assumed that the Bruch No. 1 concerto was already in place and that all I had to do was switch on. I did so, and turned to leave the room. I would telephone for the doctor.

It was another CD that had been left in the machine. The understated opening strokes of the Prelude to *Tristan und Isolde* called me back. I turned to change the CD.

Anna stopped me. 'It's all right, Gregushka. Please leave that on'.

I went through and rang to leave a message asking our doctor to call.

When I returned, Anna was lying motionless, eyes closed, lips fashioned in an elegant reminder of her smile. The sunlight on her face lent it a quality that, for all her beauty, I had never seen there before.

I sat on the bed, leaned down and slipped Anna into my arms. Over and over, I kissed her cheeks, her throat, her forehead.

Burning tears were dampening Anna's face. I realized that they came from me, and lifted my head.

Anna opened her eyes, looked into mine.

I could not have moved if I had wanted to. All that she had told me, pieced together from the fragmental revelations of well over a year, ran through my mind.

Anna's father was Lavrenti Beria, under Stalin head of the NKVD, or KGB, as it was later renamed. Beria's amusement was to trawl the streets of Moscow, or any other city where he happened to be, looking for women to rape.

Anna's mother, a lawyer, had been widowed for about three years when she became one of those whom Beria dragged off the sidewalk into his limousine.

Her professional expertise and experience gave her, so she believed, all the means to bring charges against Beria. Her efforts were blocked, and she found herself effectively disbarred. It was only because Beria's power was then on the wane (he was shot just weeks later) that she escaped arrest.

Once she was certain of being pregnant, Anna's mother at first considered having the foetus aborted. Because of a weakness in her condition, her gynaecologist warned that the undertaking might well prove fatal.

Though she no longer had any wish to live, her death would have meant a state orphanage for Alexander, who was then only eight years old. Not wishing the boy to grow up with only the Soviet Government for a parent, the poor woman decided against abortion.

One thing was apparent: Anna's mother had never in any way treated her daughter as an unwanted or resented child. Anna when I first met her was a normal, joyful, playful fourteen-year-old, self-assured and with eyes open for the wonders of life.

It was Alexander who knew the dreadful secret and who told it to Anna, with the Colonel's approval, when she reached sixteen. The knowledge unleashed in Anna such hatred of the Soviet system, and of the KGB in particular, that, as I remember well, the Colonel had spoken of her 'fanaticism'.

Clearly, the outrage against his mother had sparked the same hatred in Alexander. Both had dedicated their lives to helping bring about the downfall of the Soviet régime.

Anna – and this, I thought, was perhaps a naturally feminine way of looking at things – had seen the enemy not in ideological, but in personal terms. It was individuals, leaders who had committed the barbarities, and it was individuals, leaders, who must pay. The crime against her mother had to be avenged.

By deliberate exercise of all the charm that she possessed – and it was considerable – Anna flattered and came to know a steadily increasing number of men holding leading positions in Soviet government. It started, in the normal course of her duties, with meetings and receptions at the Ministry of Foreign Affairs. Contacts made on these occasions brought in invitations to other ministerial functions, leading Anna into ever higher echelons of power as her circle of acquaintances and her popularity grew.

Brezhnev she had come to know surprisingly quickly. Her name began to appear with such regularity on Kremlin invitation lists that she had to remind herself that she was in Moscow not to fraternize with the enemy, but to strike a blow at him.

In due course, Anna became a privileged spectator when Brezhnev appeared as usual at the annual parade in Red Square. In the evening, she was invited to the customary reception at the Kremlin.

It was usual for guests to take some sort of gift for their hosts. Anna had frequently left bottles of whisky at parties she had attended. This time she handed over a bottle of cask strength malt whisky as a gift for Leonid Brezhnev, host of the occasion and a strong drinker.

I did not know that Anna had taken with her to Moscow the second bottle that we had bought before our wedding. I can, on the other hand, easily imagine the subtle, insinuating way in which she would point out that a real man would tip a glassful down in one go.

Rightly, Anna expected all such gifts to be tested for toxicity. None would be found in any of the whisky that she had presented over the few years of her time in Moscow. Nonetheless, a full glass of cask strength malt would, as I had told her, stop the heart if tossed down in the manner of vodka.

Whatever the sequence of events, the fact is that three days later Brezhnev's heart gave out.

'Thanks to you, Gregushka', Anna told me with a first return of that mischievous smile of hers, 'I learned that whisky could be the proverbial blunt instrument'.

Brezhnev's successor, Yuri Andropov, had for the preceding fifteen years been head of the KGB, and thus not only Brezhnev's but also one of Beria's successors. He was indeed the KGB's longest serving head.

Without my knowledge, Anna had once again bought bottles of cask strength single malt during a previous home leave. She presented one of these to Andropov at the only reception of his that she attended after his appointment as General Secretary of the Communist Party of the Soviet Union. Andropov was admitted to hospital with total renal failure. 'It seems', Anna commented to me, 'that too much alcohol can knock out kidneys as well'.

Andropov never left hospital. He conducted the business of state from his bed, which he left only when lifted onto a couch while the sheets were changed.

I cannot say whether Anna really had succeeded in assassinating two leaders of the Soviet Union. I know only that she was convinced of it and believed that she had satisfactorily avenged her mother. Many will argue *Post hoc, non propter hoc,* and of course I am unable to contradict this.

'It was all my own idea', Anna told me. 'His majesty knew nothing'.

Just like my abduction of Dolores.

Anna was disappointed at having been unable to draw close to Andropov's successor.

Konstantin Tchernenko was unwell even as he succeeded to the General Secretaryship of the party.

Before there could be any occasion for Anna to present Tchernenko with *A Gift from Bonnie Scotland,* he was hospitalized for a month. Next, his doctors sent him away to a spa town. This scarcely helped. While there, he contracted pneumonia. Like Andropov, Tchernenko spent the last months of his life in hospital.

Before Tchernenko died, Anna was arrested. She was never told why. Her own theory was that poison was suspected in her gift to Andropov, and very possibly a connection supposed with Brezhnev's death as well.

It seems significant that officials from our embassy were not allowed to visit her. This was an unusual step, suggesting the gravest possible suspicions against her.

In the Lubyanka, Anna was subjected to the same sort of round and round routine interrogation that I had undergone at headquarters.

Who gave you the whisky?

What was in the whisky?

Was it in the whisky when it was given to you, or did you add it yourself?

Did your controller give you something to add to the whisky?

What is the name of your controller?

Is your husband your controller?

Did your controller give you the whisky?

Did your husband give you the whisky?

How many bottles did your controller give you?

To whom did he tell you to give it?

Does your controller give you whisky every time you go home?

Do you ever give whisky to people in the United Kingdom?

Did Rollerskate give you the whisky?

That was unexpected. Rollerskate had been one of our most experienced men, a legend in the Service. He had however been already retired for some time. Evidently Moscow did not know this, which was unaccountable. Both sides usually knew in some detail the teams to which they were opposed. Rollerskate had been succeeded by a versatile top man codenamed Gosling. It was surprising that Moscow was still in the dark about this.

Anna told me that she was subjected to around a week of questioning about whisky generally, with never any mention of strength and without the name of either Brezhnev or Andropov.

This was surprising, both to Anna and myself. We were compelled to assume that the KGB did not have even an empty bottle left, and that its investigators were working without evidence on the theory of an undetectable poison.

Not until some years later did I learn from one of our Kremlin sources that a member of Andropov's staff had taken a drink from the same bottle and suffered a non-fatal heart attack. This, it appears, was what had eventually alerted the KGB.

In time, it seems, they realized that they had nothing to go on, and gave up.

Once they had relinquished whisky as a topic, Anna's questioners went on to routine interrogation about the Service. Here, of course, Anna could tell them nothing, because she knew nothing.

With questioning finally abandoned, Anna was systematically abused by her guards. Frankly, this surprised me. I believed that rank and file KGB personnel were subject to stringent discipline. Years of abuse were the origin of Anna's infection with HIV.

I now understood the true reason that Moscow had agreed to the exchange. Not, as I had thought, to get their own people back, but in order to rid themselves of a prisoner who was HIV positive. Let the West have the burden of such people – that would be their stance.

The music from the CD subsided, caught its breath, flowed into Isolde's spirit-wrenching *Liebestod.*

Anna's smile deepened. With measureless slowness, her eyes drifted to a close.

I felt Anna's fingers press lightly into the backs of my shoulders.

This was the last exercise of what little strength Anna had left.

Gossamer-light, her hands slipped from my back into limpness. I thought I heard a sigh.

I leaned forward and kissed Anna's lips. My tears were falling onto her again.

The smile was still on her face.

Anna looked as young and as sublimely beautiful as she had been when I was first reintroduced to her at Twelvetrees.

I did not concede my hold on Anna's lifeless form until my tears were exhausted and the final protracted chords of the *Liebestod* were an echo hovering in the memory.

She was too young, far too young. Yet I knew that it was not how long we lived that mattered, but what we did and how we comported ourselves during our lives.

Shakespeare was both right and wrong when at his most dismissive:

> *We are such stuff*
> *As dreams are made on; and our little life*
> *Is rounded with a sleep.*

Gordon Lang

THE NAZI GENE

By the same author:
The Carnoustie Effect/Warfare in the 21st Century
For Führer, Folk and Fatherland
The Giftie
The Half Sister

(in German):
Die Polen verprügeln, vols. 1&2
Das perestrojanische Pferd

Gordon Lang
The Nazi Gene
©2012 Conflict Books, London E3
All rights reserved
Printed in the UK 2012 by anchorprint.co.uk
ISBN 978-0-9558240-1-2

THE
NAZI GENE

Conflict

I

THERE is a little bit of Nazi in every one of us. Oh, I do beg your pardon. Not in you, of course. Nor in any member of your family.

But in everyone else.

I don't mean just some tendency to let any slight authority go straight to one's head (becoming a 'little Hitler', as we used to call it). Real Naziness is in those so utterly convinced of the exclusive rightness of their beliefs that they dismiss with unmitigated contempt all who disagree with them – and hail as marvellously clever fellows any who share their views.

It is almost a law of nature that those boasting themselves most 'liberal' turn out to be the most intolerant. Lovers of all humanity, every one. Until they run into someone having an outlook different from theirs. Let anyone contradict these paragons on any point, and they will make the poor fellow appear and feel as though he is next door to being a criminal.

That is their inner Nazi at work.

And for real hostility, try those ubiquitous disciples of universal brotherhood, the 'peace' demonstrators.

Of course, Naziness did not arise only with the birth of the Nazi movement. There was simply no name for it before Hitler, though it has been working its havoc as long as humankind has had speech and the ability to reason.

It inspired the Spanish Inquisition, ignited the Thirty Years' War and propelled Oliver Cromwell into his career of fanatical self-righteousness and suppression. It presided over the Terror of the French revolution, motivated and prompted at the elbows of Lenin and Stalin.

What we can all recognize as Naziness – treating opponents with inhuman contempt – crops up every bit as virulently among those who are, nominally, its greatest ideological opponents. Look at Stalin and his purges of Jews.

Among us now it is as active as ever. In individuals the spring of acrimony and font of disharmony, in governments a global menace. Through simple nurture of our universal Nazi gene, leaders can rear a whole nation into intolerant self-assurance. Trouble is not then long in coming.

When I left the Service to look after my dying wife, I believed – wrongly – that I had left all that behind. The Service dragged me back with no warning beyond a telephone call just before dawn. At the other end of the line the voice was courteous, unmistakeably official and quite unknown to me. 'Can you hold yourself ready to receive a visit at 9am?'

I could and, though I did not say so, would welcome the variety in my day.

It was probably the very first ring of the phone that had woken me. Since Anna died, I don't seem able to go into any very deep sleep. The least sound wakes me.

I had lifted the telephone before putting on any light. Now I switched on a lamp, swung my legs on to the floor, padded towards the shower and set about making myself fit to receive visitors.

Anyone preparing to arrive in Argyll by nine o'clock, I told myself, would be something of an early riser. That suggested a matter of some importance. Not another missing agent, I hoped.

The sound of an approaching helicopter at about half past eight alerted me, but the machine passed overhead. No decent landing place here, of course.

At a couple of minutes to nine, a detective superintendent rang at my door. The man was of imposing stature and spoke in a pleasant baritone.

'Ian Baxter Greig?'

Apart from the fact that this sounded too much like the preliminary to arrest, the man's clothes shouted out unmistakably that he was a policeman. His was not as obvious as the old Gestapo 'plain clothes' uniform of full length leather overcoat and floppy-brimmed trilby, but a policeman's idea of anonymity, nonetheless.

I took my caller into what my mother had insisted on calling her withdrawing room. Here were our most comfortable chairs, reserved solely for visitors.

The superintendent declined to take advantage of these. 'If you are agreeable, sir', he began, 'I am to take you at once to Craigard'.

My knowledge of Gaelic was patchy – just enough to understand that Craigard meant High Rock. What I knew beyond that was the significance of the island, and despite my being fully content in early retirement the thought of it excited me.

Whatever was amiss on Craigard, it would be something that no one else wanted to touch, something either insoluble or pointless. That could be the only explanation for their calling me in.

How often I had been required to sign the Official Secrets Act, or an addendum relating to a specific task! The superintendent had one ready for me now, and I committed myself with a joy that I had not expected to feel. My days since Anna's death, I now realized, had become as empty as they could be.

Old habits, good or bad, are notoriously hard to discard. Throughout my years in the Service, including my married ones, I had kept near my bed a bag filled with essentials sufficient for a number of impromptu overnight stays. Whenever the call should come, I was always ready for a quick start.

The Russian composer Dmitri Shostakovich had also slept with a packed case ready, in case of a 3am visit by Stalin's secret police. Once I heard of this, I ever afterwards thought of my own stand-by kit as my 'Shostakovich bag'. It was beside my bed now and inside five minutes I followed the superintendent out of the door with it.

Only six months earlier I should have turned down flat any request to step back into harness. I had cut all ties and, except with the Colonel, had no communication with anyone in the Service. Nor did I wish for any. That, at least, was what I had told myself. Six months ago.

A letter from Johnston had changed all that. I had not seen my old school friend since we were both nineteen. We had exchanged Christmas cards, and that was all. Then a letter from Johnston had torn me out of the lethargy into which I had plunged after Anna's death. Johnston had lost his wife to cancer, and in giving me the news wrote of the difficulty that he was having in rebuilding his life.

These words had woken my conscience. Johnston was a chap whom I had always regarded as rather timid, whereas I was supposed to be the man of action. Yet here was Johnston talking about rebuilding his life, while since my own wife's death I had never once thought in such terms. There was no denying the fact. I had simply been drifting. I was still young enough to pursue any number of undertakings, yet without excuse had abandoned all active life.

Johnston had put me to shame. If he could rebuild...

My first step had been to publish a memoir of Anna. While she was at Britain's Moscow embassy, Anna had struck blows at the Soviet leadership off her own bat. She had returned to Britain from Soviet imprisonment suffering from HIV, and I had resigned from the Service to nurse her.

After Anna's death, I sold our Home Counties house and returned to my childhood home in Argyll.

Within a year, my mother too had died, peacefully in her sleep.

Writing Anna's story had caused me no little embarrassment. I had found it necessary to write in the first person, and this went distinctly against the grain. The work would, I feared, appear narcissistic. As it turned out, the exercise had served as a wonderful catharsis. Nothing could erase the pain of Anna's death, but writing openly about the experience seemed to have aided me in struggling through my grief.

In those early days after Anna's death, every ring of the telephone had infuriated me for dragging my mind from memories or dreams of Anna.

Too long, I saw now, I had been living in a perpetuation of my misery. It had taken the need to send Johnston a sympathetic reply to drag me out of it and return me to the world of practicalities.

Now the telephone was no longer an invader to be cursed, but a friend to be welcomed. The superintendent's visit was a blessing, giving me something besides self-pity to occupy my mind.

After having idled so greatly and squandered so much time, I was finally finding myself in a return to action.

Once, a policeman's car would have been British – a Wolseley, usually. Or a Humber. Was I becoming small-minded in regretting that I was being asked to step into the product of an overseas country that not long since had been our enemy?

Whatever its origin, the car was quiet, stable and comfortable. It was hard to believe that the superintendent's driver, a Londoner, was a newcomer to Highland roads. Through mile after mile of Argyll's bends and curves he displayed an infallible touch. Within a quarter of an hour, he brought us to a rocky clearing where he pulled smoothly off the road.

Here a Special Branch helicopter was waiting with its single rotor resting fore and aft, as if on parade. Apart from this precision there was nothing to suggest any Service connection. The machine carried a civilian registration number on its sky blue fuselage. Such a contrast to those shiny black FBI 'copters, flaunting the bureau's initials intimidatingly huge in white.

Our machine could have been one of those executive playthings used by businessmen to fly themselves and their guests from golf course to golf course. And, of course, to advertise their owners as Important Men.

The owner in this case was HM Government, and if the machine were ever to land at a golf course it would be on the trail of villainy, not in a quest for tee times.

The pilot, in civilian clothes, lifted the machine at once. Before swinging onto course for Craigard he took her to an altitude greater than I had expected.

The superintendent whistled. 'That's some beach. What do you call it? The Scottish Riviera?'

He was looking towards the south, where the long sands off Machrihanish had become brilliant in the sunlight. Not for a moment could I be deceived by the illusion of idyll. I never saw those sands or heard a mention of the place without feeling in phantom detail the powerlessness of my young boy's legs and arms, my mouth full of salt, the choking sea flooding into my nose.

'Don't be fooled', I told him. 'The sea is never to be underestimated. And especially here'.

'Why particularly here?'

'In a direct line, there is nothing between those sands and Newfoundland. When the ocean's in the mood, we can feel the full power of Atlantic rollers'.

Those boyhood images of helpless sinking in the waves would never leave me. Nor would my gratitude to the unexpected roller that had flung me in closely enough to the beach for me to touch bottom with a toe. With the assistance of a making tide, I had been able somehow to struggle to shore. An ebb would have dragged me the other way. Since then, I have had enormous respect for the sea and the power of its waves. I count that early experience as a blessing. It protected me from later foolhardiness.

II

'GOOD lord! I see what you mean'. As our helicopter swung onto its north westerly course, the superintendent's eye had been caught by a patch of sea off the northernmost tip of Jura, apparently boiling like the contents of a kettle.

'That', I told him, 'is Corrievreckan, the world's third largest whirlpool'.

'Heavens! I shouldn't like to see numbers one and two'.

In 1820, Corrievreckan had wrecked the world's first passenger steamer, Comet. Locals knew that it had also very nearly deprived the world of Nineteen Eight Four when it came close to drowning a Jura resident named Eric Blair, otherwise calling himself George Orwell.

I looked from the vortex below to the tip of Ardnamurchan, the most westerly point of mainland Britain. Years before, I had thought that I might build a retirement home on the peninsula for Anna and myself. I had negotiated for some land, and gone as far as having a man from the local council travel out from Fort William to meet me on the site to discuss the provision of drainage and a water supply.

The KGB had put paid to all such notions, yet now I wondered whether if Anna had lived I might not have dropped the project anyway. With my mother ageing and alone, a return to my childhood home had much to be said for it.

All these memories and reflections were swept aside by a rising – no, not euphoria; that would be too strong a word, and an overworked one at that. Happiness? Not strong enough. What wrapped itself round me as we headed for Craigard was plain and simple joy. A blissful delight such as, after Anna's death, I had never expected to experience again. By the time Benbecula and the Uists had slipped away behind us, animated curiosity had distilled into impatience for whatever lay in wait for me at Craigard.

On the picture postcards and the calendars, what lay a thousand feet below us would, I knew, be a carpet of unrelieved blue. Yet nature disdained to imitate art. The North Atlantic vastness remained leaden.

Ahead, a darker spot, cast iron. A spot with a skirt of lace. Lace that crashed into its sides, then flew into the air. Lace with a life of its own, battering on all sides an island that stood alone and friendless, almost fifty miles west of the Outer Hebrides.

Places, like people, frequently look better from a distance than they do close up. Craigard was one of the exceptions. As we neared for our landing, I could see that less than half of the island's surface was covered with the grey-painted buildings, tarmac and concrete that gave it such a forbidding appearance from afar. Most of the rock – and the island is scarcely more than that – glowed rich with the more familiar Highland mixture of green, yellow, purple and brown.

I had never before seen so many sea birds in one place. Puffins, fulmars, gannets, petrels – all rose in great animated blankets that wheeled away as we dropped towards them.

The pilot spun our machine round – to face upwind, was it? – before settling her as gently as possible in what was clearly something more than a summer breeze. That there was always a substantial wind here was something that I was to learn.

Three men were waiting for us on the tarmac. While two were obvious ground crew ready to take care of the helicopter, the third stood alone. He wore an Army uniform with the shoulder crowns of a major. I took him to be the head of the establishment, but in this was mistaken. The police superintendent, following me down from the machine, introduced us.

'Major Jardine, Ian Greig'.

Jardine's handshake was warm, his eyes frank and confident. 'Delighted to have you with us', he told me.

I could only hope that the Service hadn't 'sold' me to the institution as some kind of miracle worker. Jardine, it turned out, was Craigard's head of security. A robust man with a reassuring presence, he radiated inner strength coupled with unflappable resolution. Whatever was the trouble here, it looked to me as though they already had the right man to deal with it.

The police superintendent was due to fly back after dealing with some routine paperwork, so he said goodbye to me at once.

'We'll get you settled in', Jardine told me, 'then we'll go and see the brigadier'.

'Settling me in' took all of five minutes. The room allocated to me was one of a dozen in a grey, single-storey barracks-like building. Craigard's security was in the hands of a detachment drawn from the Army. These quarters were for its handful of officers.

I did no more than rinse my hands, splash my face and run a brush and comb through my hair. I was ready for the brigadier.

The island of Craigard, otherwise uninhabited for the past hundred years, was home to Britain's Advanced Weapons Research and Test Facility. It had not occurred to me that the establishment might be run by the Army rather than by whatever collection of boffins did the research. Certainly though, placing it in the hands of one of the Armed Services made sense. I remembered that Peenemünde, birthplace of both the cruise missile and the rocket, was originally a German Army institution until being taken over by the SS in its later days.

There was little conspicuous about the military presence on Craigard. Just two low barracks buildings, an administration block, an ammunition store, a radar station and a sonar hut, all painted battleship grey, plus an anti-aircraft gun emplacement with a 'roof' of grey netting. Those laboratories and workshops that were not underground, sited away from the Army buildings, were similarly unobtrusive. From the air, as I had seen for myself, camouflage was effective. It was the immense colonies of sea birds that caught the eye.

Considering the low strength of the unit stationed on the island, it might be thought astonishing that a brigadier, normally in command of two regiments, had been assigned to run the establishment. Yet the CO's task lay primarily in overseeing the weapons research. The security detachment was Jardine's responsibility.

He was also effectively the CO's adjutant, occupying the brigadier's outer office.

Brigadier Dickson was a strongly built man of something like six foot four or five, largely bald and with penetrating dark eyes. His handshake was brisk, his manner courteous but business-like.

'Well, Greig, I dare say you'll get to the bottom of this affair. Anything you need, Jardine'll fix you up'.

That was all. I still had no idea what 'this affair' was.

'He won't want to be bothered with any of the details', Jardine warned me once we had left. 'He'll just want to know the result when there is one'.

That suited me. I was used to operating alone, and had always resented the necessity of submitting daily activity reports when there was no tangible progress to be noted.

'I'll show you how much we've learned so far', said Jardine. He smiled. 'Not very much, actually. Perhaps, though, you should start with the doc'.

The medical officer, Captain Naismith, was a stocky, fair haired man of medium height. He ruled over a consulting room and a three-bed sick bay. So far as I was capable of assessing it, the equipment at his disposal included sophisticated devices of recent design. 'He's here for the boffins as well, of course', Jardine told me, 'not just for our boys'.

Generators built into the rock – one in round-the-clock use, a second in reserve – provided power for everything on the island. This included, to my astonishment, a freezer casket for a cadaver.

'I'm to let you have a look at him before we send him away', said Naismith.

He opened the lid of the casket and I saw the body of a man – an obvious Oriental – on whom a complete autopsy had been performed. He had been stitched back together, with even the top of his cranium replaced.

Naismith showed me the man's brain, but it meant nothing to me. What on earth was I supposed to see? Surely all brains looked alike, so why had he bothered to cut out this one? Twenty seven bullets in the body, including two in the heart, spoke for themselves. Not one shot had as much as grazed the man's head, so why take it to pieces?

'Here', said the MO. 'Underneath. This almond shaped thing. That's where he had a flaw, in the amygdala. That's why he gave our chaps so much trouble'.

The man leaned back to let me move in and take a closer look. I was hanged if I wanted to see the thing, but made a polite effort and peered at the place that he indicated. Frankly, I found the whole thing distasteful. There was no need for me to see a dead man's brain. At least, that was what I felt at the time.

If I had wanted to mess around with this sort of thing, I should have gone to medical school. The reason I did not pursue such a path was that I never cared for the idea of taking intimate looks at other folks' bodies, never mind handling them. Not even when they were alive. Looking at their insides after death appealed to me even less.

Captain Naismith, on the other hand, seemed proud of his work – and why, in fairness, shouldn't he be? It was a good thing that we had people to do this sort of thing. The man was clearly as pleased as Punch at what he had found.

'See those lesions? They're what did it. Doubt if he was born that way, but Heaven knows what happened to do that sort of damage'.

Despite myself, I was curious. 'Why couldn't he have been born that way?'

'Because if he had been, he wouldn't have survived his childhood, that's why. This little thing...'

'What was it? The amyg...?'

'The amygdala, yes. Not just the shape of an almond, but only the size of one, too. This is what we depend on to tell us when we should be afraid. It processes our observations and gives us warning. Anyone born with a damaged one would charge out in front of a bus as soon as he was able to walk'.

'In effect, then, it is a safety mechanism?'

'Very much so. Without it, the human species would never have survived'.

Well, the fellow in this casket had obviously done a decent job of surviving. By the look of him, he had made it well into his thirties. He had then come practically half way round the globe (or was he born here?) and evidently given our chaps a deal of trouble before being downed.

'Who is he?' I asked.

'We've no idea', Jardine admitted.

159

'No papers on him at all, I suppose?'

'None'.

'Printing of any kind – for example on clothes labels?'

'Nothing there, either'.

'Tattoos?'

'Not a mark'.

'How did...?'

'Sorry. We know neither where he came from, nor how he managed to land here'.

'Well', I pointed out, 'we know how he didn't land here'.

Naismith and Jardine looked at me.

'He didn't arrive by parachute. If he had, there would be markings on him from the rubbing of his harness, sore spots that can take several days to fade. There is nothing of the kind here, neither under his arms nor anywhere else'.

Jardine nodded. 'Sea, then?'

'Had to be'.

I knew where I was now. They had sent for me because they had an intruder who was a complete mystery. A case that was nothing but blanks, and I was expected to fill in all of them. Very nice.

III

HAD the Service wanted to lure me out of retirement by giving me a tasty case to whet my appetite? This seemed unlikely, since I was scarcely popular with anyone at the top of the firm. Far from fitting in, I was regarded generally as an outsider, and certainly as a stiff-necked prig.

Distaste was a two-way thing. There were some of my fellow officers whom I could not help seeing as overgrown schoolboys, however effective they were at their jobs. I made no use of the puerile euphemisms and circumlocutions popular among senior grades, but called everything, including Headquarters and the Service itself, by its proper name.

No one would be eager to have me back. If, on the other hand, they needed what the Americans call a patsy to fall flat on his face and look a general all-round idiot...

Apart from this, I could well imagine that, with everyone working at full stretch on anti-terrorist intelligence, no one in the Service could be spared for investigating any odd cases. And here, in the freezer casket, was an undisputable oddity. No one would want an assignment like this, and Headquarters doubtless felt it preferable to see an emeritus flounder round uselessly in the mud, rather than one of its latest generation of bright boys.

'Clothes?' I asked.

Everything the man had on him was neatly packed into a box ready to send off with the corpse for detailed laboratory examination. That should reveal the origin of the materials. The man's clothing was lightweight but water-resistant. So too were his boots. He had worn a waist belt of 9mm ammunition and carried an FN-Browning pistol, a Swiss Army watch and penknife, a small Norwegian compass, a digital camera and a telephone that was almost as bulky as one of the old two-way radios – walkie-talkies as they were called. A memory card was in a slot in the telephone. A rucksack that would hold all of his equipment, including his clothing, was one hundred per cent waterproof.

A water bottle and a small plastic box containing one blue pill completed his equipment. Both camera and telephone were waterproof, though the camera's usefulness had been ended by two bullets. Unlike most pistols, which took a magazine of eight shots, the FN-Browning carried thirteen. Only six were left in this one. The barrel had not been cleaned after firing. The watch, also waterproof, was still functioning.

'Any of our boys hurt?'

'Thank goodness, no', Jardine responded. 'They had him well surrounded, all from solid cover, before challenging him with a warning shot. I'm amazed he managed to get off as many as seven rounds. He hit nothing but rocks, though'.

'No chance of taking him alive?'

'None, I'm afraid. He just stood up and charged'.

'Charged?'

'Flat out, straight into our gun barrels. Like a hero in a Western film. Absolutely no sense to it'.

'Where was this?'

'Just off the beach, where there's quite a slope. I'll show you the spot later. Lots of gorse there, all the way up. He could easily have gone to ground, and it would have taken some time to track him down. Meanwhile, he could have been picking off our chaps from excellent cover. Yet he just came straight for us. It made no sense at all'.

'Do you think he meant to be killed?'

'Suicide?' Jardine became thoughtful. 'Yes, I'm afraid in retrospect it does rather look like that'.

I turned to Naismith. 'Have you had a look at that blue pill?'

'A look, yes. I haven't the means here for analysis'.

'But you have an idea?'

The captain pursed his lips. 'Shouldn't want to commit myself, but it looks like an L-pill'.

I agreed. A lethal pill. A lifetime ago, we had given those to the agents we sent in behind German lines.

In this case the man had not had time to take out and swallow his pill. He preferred the simpler option of running into our boys' fire. It had certainly worked. Twenty seven bullet wounds. They had damned nearly cut him in half. A miracle that the telephone had survived.

Now why on earth, in the middle of peace, would anyone send in a man seemingly with orders to kill himself if he were discovered? Was he not expected to return? Is that why there was one item that he did not have among his equipment: money? No currency of any kind was found on the man's body.

If he did not die, were there plans to evacuate him? If so, the man would presumably have left by the same means as when he had arrived. By sea. Yet how had any vessel slipped in close enough even once to be undetected? To try it again would certainly be sticking out necks. For hostile espionage services there was no more tempting target than our advanced weapons establishment, save only for the Americans' equivalent. Yet only a top-ranking country could, or would, have possessed both the means and the audacity to launch such an operation.

Who had sent this man with a one-way ticket? Watch, knife and pistol were European, camera and telephone Japanese. I was willing to bet that his clothing would turn out to be Japanese, too. This did not mean that I suspected the man himself of being Japanese, or that the Japanese had sent him. Since 1945, the Japs have been reluctant to operate any spy rings abroad, for fear of arousing diplomatic complications. I thought it more likely that the dead man was Chinese, and that in kitting him out his masters had naturally taken care that he would carry nothing that could be traced back to China.

I took the box with the man's belongings along to Jardine's office. There I subjected every item to as thorough an examination as was possible without laboratory equipment. I searched for anything hidden or sewn into fabrics, any conceivable place of concealment in the boots, watch, knife, camera or telephone. There were no labels on the clothing, no markings on either the outsides or the insides of his boots. Watch, camera, knife and telephone could have been bought anywhere. I was puzzled, though, by the bulkiness of the telephone. It must have been awkward to carry in a pocket, and was an odd choice when the man could have packed something like ten or a dozen of the latest neat mobile devices into the same space. Unlike the telephone, the now unusable camera had no memory card in its slot.

Despite his undeniable ethnicity, the man could even have been a British citizen. He could also have been a lone wolf, not working for anyone's intelligence service but merely indulging in some speculative adventuring on his own account. This, though, I considered highly unlikely.

There was one clue, and one clue only, as to who might have sent the man. Even this was only a potential clue, nothing more. It was in the radio frequency to which his telephone was tuned. We were, fortunately, on an island thick with boffins. It would be a poor state of affairs if no one could discover what that frequency was. A telephone like this one would not have the power to reach China. I doubted, too, whether it could reach a satellite to bounce the pictures on to China. It could, though, reach London and the Chinese Embassy. Our technical boys must know what frequencies the embassy used. They would know all the frequencies favoured by other countries' secret services.

'Let's have the leading radio man in here', I told Jardine. 'You must have a compatible cable somewhere. We need to plug in the telephone and keep the battery charged up. We'll leave it switched on; something might come in. And fix up a recorder. The more we can get on tape, the better our chances of breaking any cypher'.

'Will do'.

I did not believe that we should receive any messages. Standard practice required the agent in the field to call in first, before his base would break its silence. Without knowing the dead man's call sign, we could do nothing but wait in unsubstantiated hope.

There was still one matter on which I was uncertain, but before I occupied my mind with this I authorized despatch to our laboratory boys of the corpse and all of his possessions save for the telephone. I also took the dead man's fingerprints and sent these off with a request that our police rope Interpol in to the search. Officially, we wanted to identify just an ordinary criminal.

'We can't get anything out of the camera', said Jardine, 'but I've printed out all the pics on the memory card. All exterior shots in the semi-dark'.

'Nothing inside any building?'

'No, I'm happy to say'.

'And the card was in the telephone?'

'Yes'.

'So the pictures had presumably already been sent. There was not another card in the camera?'

'Not another anywhere'.

I laid out the photographs that Jardine had printed. There was an obvious order to them. Our Chinese friend, if that's what he was, had been a man of method. Placed side by side, the images gave four complementary panoramic views of the island establishment, from due south, west, north and finally due east. No building had been missed, not the boathouse with its three motor launches, nor even the one-man spotter's post that had been established on an eminence a good half-mile from the AA gun. The layouts of both research establishment and army camp were crystal-clear.

'It looks', explained Jardine, 'as though he were sending the pictures from his telephone when our warning shot interrupted him'.

'Or he did not begin to send them until your warning shot prompted him into action?' I wondered. 'Alternatively, he had already sent them off beforehand. How did you get on to him?'

'Thermal imaging. We have thermal image cameras sweeping the laboratory area'.

'And your camp?'

'None there'.

'Not covering the AA gun, either?'

'No'.

Compilation of panoramic views was all very well, but surely the Chinese already knew the layout of Craigard from their satellite pictures, not to mention high-altitude flights. Commercial passenger aircraft – and freight carriers, too – flying between continents routinely carried spy cameras.

Only for a direct assault would one require the sort of detail captured by a camera on the ground.

'Have you', I asked Jardine, 'already shown this lot to the brigadier?'

'Not yet. It was only early last night that we caught the man. I wrote my report and gave that to the brigadier, then watched Naismith doing his autopsy. I didn't get round to developing the pictures until shortly before you arrived'.

'Well, let's show them to the CO now'.

Brigadier Dickson looked, and said little. 'All right, Jardine. We know now what the fellow was doing. Someone wants to bomb us out of existence. Well, I must leave it to you two to find out who'.

You two? This was just what had been puzzling me. What had I to contribute at Jardine's side that someone else could not? The Army had its own intelligence branch. Why had someone not been fetched from there? MI5 was responsible for national security, and my police visitor showed that Special Branch had already been brought in. Why had it been thought necessary to contact my own Service as well, to prise me out of comfortable retirement like a winkle from its shell?

As it happened, I had responded readily enough, but there was no way that Headquarters could have foreseen this. The question remained. Why send for me, when the Army could have carried out its own investigation? It seemed to me unnatural for the Army, for MI5, or for Special Branch, to let an outsider into one of their cases. There was normally such rivalry between services that officers guarded their own data as closely as a young girl concealing confessions of a secret love in her diary.

IV

THOUGH I had next to no expectation of receiving a call on the intruder's telephone, I asked Headquarters to send an Oriental languages expert at once.

She was promised for the following day, a Japanese girl who had been recruited by our Embassy in Tokyo and had served at our Shanghai Station. Her name, we were told, was Millie. That was just about all that we ever learned about her.

The battery of the intruder's telephone had been fully charged, and one of our boffins rigged up a device that would enable its working frequency to be read out, should a call come in. When or if it did, the voice-activated recorder should give us something for Millie to work on. Unless, of course, any message was encrypted into just a series of numbers. Oddly, this did not seem too probable, since among the dead man's kit was nothing that could be used as a deciphering tool. The man would have needed to carry everything in his head. Not impossible, of course.

Meanwhile I examined all the systems protecting the island. As was to be expected at the nation's most sensitive and valuable establishment, radar cover was of the highest standard. Jardine saw to it that the single anti-aircraft gun, whose crew had been on permanent stand-by, was now kept in round-the-clock readiness, with crews on a rota system. Many commercial flights passed at great heights directly over Craigard, or on paths close to being directly above. At irregular intervals, Jardine would use a radar sighting of one of these flights to stage a gun drill. These showed that he had kept his men in a high state of efficiency. They were as well trained as any unit one was likely to encounter in the Army. Jardine himself impressed with his unruffled competence and thoughtful disposition.

His soldiers were at less than company strength, with two machine guns alongside the usual assault rifles and hand guns. I was appalled to find that they had no night vision goggles, and went to the brigadier with an immediate demand for these.

'I put in an indent four or five months ago', Jardine told me. 'They'll send them now that we've had an intruder'.

We never had a chance to find out whether they would. The truth was that not even a second anti-aircraft gun would have been of use if Jardine were expected to defend the island against attack from the air. When research laboratories were first established on Craigard, MoD thinking was still at World War Two level. This was reflected in the quality and extent of the defences thought necessary: an infantry company to repel a commando raid, an AA gun to deal with any bomber. More than a half-century later, what would the Chinese – or anyone else – deploy against the UK's most advanced facility? There would be no bombing raid in the conventional sense. Today's ultra-accurate missiles could be programmed to penetrate a building at any chosen point, such as a door, window or grating. Defence against these was possible only by means of anti-missile missiles – or better still by preventing the attacker from launching his missiles altogether. Failing these capabilities, Craigard was literally without defence.

'It's like', commented Jardine, 'trying to contain hydrochloric acid in a brown paper bag'.

While it was true that Jardine was expected to conduct active defence of the island with outdated means, there was nothing inadequate about the passive defence measures taken to protect the establishment. All laboratories and most test facilities were located in tunnels bored well underground. These, it was expected, would withstand even medium size atomic weapons. Exposed on the surface were accommodation blocks, our radar station and the workshops where jigs, patterns, scale models, simulators and the occasional prototype were fabricated. There was also a test stand for firing out to sea.

'Someone wants to bomb us out of existence', the brigadier had said. This was certainly what the intruder's photographs suggested. Targets for an attack were now identified in detail.

All the same, an aircraft launching a missile at us seemed unlikely. Any aircraft not on a regular flight path and entering UK air space would be detected by our RAF friends and quickly intercepted by fighters.

A submarine, on the other hand, could launch a programmed missile from practically anywhere in the world's oceans. She need be nowhere near UK territorial waters, and so would excite no attention. She could also bring an intruder to within a mile or less of the island before surfacing and casting the man loose in a canoe. Any inflatable would do the job, of course, but a canoe has the preferred shape for moving through water quickly and in a straight line. Any Royal Marine will tell you that.

Sonar buoys and anti-submarine nets were, I discovered, positioned only off the bay, where the island had its solitary beach. Something like ninety per cent of Craigard's coastline – around twelve miles of it – remained open to hostile approach. We could at least mount a watch covering those twelve miles, though it was apparent that very few places were suitable for a landing. With cliffs, cliffs and more cliffs pretty well all the way round the island, there was no mystery about the name Craigard. From every angle except directly facing the solitary beach, the island presented voyagers with no more of a welcome than that of high and vertical rock. Most of these frontages were no less steep, and many of them no less high, than those at Dover. The difference was that Craigard was not composed of white chalk, but of igneous granite.

Jardine was a marvel. In double quick time he selected seven positions on high ground from where all of the surrounding sea could be monitored, and produced a duty roster providing for two men at each station round the clock.

Meanwhile, he organized search parties to hunt among rocks and the island's bushes for a collapsible canoe. That just might be the one item to give us a clue as to who had sent the man.

I was not optimistic of results, and considered it likely that the canoe – if one had been used – had been deliberately sunk a few yards off the coast, at a place where it could if necessary be retrieved for a return journey. Our visitor's lack of funds must mean that he had been expecting either to be fetched back to his base or to end his life here.

Jardine's quartermaster kitted me out with complete scuba gear, and I took to the water. I had an underwater camera with me and began my search at the western end of the bay below the Army camp. This was the island's sole location offering any reasonable possibility of landing. Elsewhere, our visitor would have been faced with sheer cliffs. Certainly, scaling these was feasible at some points, but I felt that anyone wanting to return to his canoe would need to have left it not only where it was accessible but also where its location could be easily marked or remembered. Logical spots seemed to me to be not directly offshore facing the beach, but a short way past one or other end of the bay, where cliffs began their ascents.

The day was wintry and the water so cold that I dived for only a minute or so at a time. Anything longer would have risked bringing on cramps – the last thing that a swimmer needs. Between plunges, I reflected wryly on those films I had seen in which all an agent's dives were into warm Caribbean waters under a glowing sun and bright blue sky. 'That', as Miss Prism comments in The Importance of Being Earnest, 'is what fiction means'.

Here was reality, and there were neither beautifully coloured fish to keep me company nor rippling seabed plants to add enchantment. Strong winds were keeping the surface lively, and an ocean swell was seeing to it that there was no peaceful time to be had a few feet down. I swept the beach from west to east by swimming out and back slowly along parallel paths. Most of these excursions were short, since in places the seabed dropped away sharply. The canoe, if there were one, would not have been abandoned to deep water, but left within reasonable swimming distance of the shore.

Small crabs were abundant, but I noticed little other life. I dare say that there were plenty of small creatures both swimming and on the floor of the sea, but having the shapes of a canoe and of canoe parts fixed in my mind, I saw right past these.

I completed my search to the farther end of the beach without having seen anything resembling a canoe. I could not leave it at that, and extended my diving past the eastern end of the bay, working my way round the headland that limited the extent of the beach. The weather was no better, and I spent some three quarters of an hour in systematic to-and-froing before my headlight caught a light object too cleanly straight not to be man-made. I propelled myself to it. There was no doubt. This was a self-inflating canoe, folded with double-bladed paddle inside.

I unhitched from my belt a length of cord and tied the loose end to the canoe. On the other end was a red rubber ball, also self-inflating. I triggered the device and let it float upwards.

As soon as I broke the surface I could see how well our visitor had chosen his spot. The location was marked now by our red rubber buoy. In addition, the intruder had practically as good an indicator in a single small tree that was growing out of the bare cliff at a crooked angle only ten or twelve feet above water level. What was more, a series of perilous but usable foot- and handholds led round the corner of the cliff that marked the eastern end of the beach.

The man had his return all worked out, then had chosen to be killed. Why?

Four of Jardine's men helped recover the canoe that afternoon. I had it taken into one of the workshops to examine it. The canoe was thoughtfully designed and well made. Clips to hold the paddle were integral and substantial. I could read nothing as to the canoe's origin, and despatched it to our Service laboratory boys. Perhaps they could identify the source of the materials used.

A message had come in for me while I was diving. I took it to my room and sat down to decipher it. The note confirmed that China Section had its hands full keeping an eye on numerous agents pursuing multiple sensitive projects in the UK. Beijing was displaying considerable interest in us. All the same, there was no information on active Chinese interest in Craigard.

It was up to me, then, to supply such knowledge.

Next, I borrowed one of the establishment's small motor boats and began a voyage right round Craigard. I took Admiralty charts with me, and on these noted all the places where fit and agile young men could mount the cliffs. Within a half mile of each of these locations, the water was deep enough for a submarine to submerge in safety. This gave any hostile force a good choice of sites for a landing.

The sun was low before I had finished, and we were treated to a Technicolor sunset straight from Disney Studios. Sun setting over the open sea is always likely to be both spectacular and memorable. This one had everything except the hero riding away into the heart of the display. Naturally, it couldn't last. Shepherd's delight, my foot! Not two hours later we were in the middle of a moonless night with total cloud cover. Keep 'em guessing – that seems to be the weather god's method.

I organized all the floodlights that I could muster – six of them – and had four arranged on the hillside, facing down so as to cover the whole width of the beach. The other two I took higher up the hillside to point in the opposite direction. None of the six was connected to our normal electrical circuit. All were to be powered by our second generator.

I ordered this to be started. The lights themselves were not to be switched on yet.

V

IT was half an hour after midnight when I fastened on a belt of ammunition, tossed a sub-machine gun, a pistol and some grenades into a jeep and prepared to drive up to the highest accessible point of the island – that is, to the highest point that I could reach without overturning the jeep on the slope.

I was planning to settle myself down at the summit and focus my binoculars on the areas of sea where an approaching submarine might surface if one were to bring a replacement for our late visitor.

Not that I could expect to see very much. Tonight there was darkness with a capital 'D'.

Before setting off, I decided to look in on our sonar crew. Normally, two ratings and a petty officer shared watches round the clock. Tonight the rating who was monitoring the screen had the detachment's CO, a lieutenant commander, looking over his shoulder.

'Good evening, sir', said the commander, straightening.

'Good evening, Whittaker'. I was uncomfortable about the 'sir', and told the man so. Technically, though, his address might have been correct. When I became one of the Service's departmental heads, the salary grade placed me equivalent to a lieutenant colonel. By inter-service comparison this ranked me just one step ahead of Whittaker. All the same, being retired I felt any reference to these matters superfluous and embarrassing.

Whittaker had been active. He had acquired a dozen or more sonar buoys – battery-powered submarine detectors made for dropping from aircraft. When they detect a submarine, these buoys send a signal back to the machine that dropped them.

Whittaker had modified the buoys by making their batteries accessible and rechargeable. Their signals he tuned for reception at his land-based station. He had then sown the buoys in a pattern covering the waters on all sides of the island.

'As long as we can keep abreast with the recharging, this will give us complete protection', Whittaker confided. 'Not defence, of course, but warning'. He had drawn up a regular rota listing the order in which buoys were to be fetched in and recharged. 'When we can fetch them in, that is. Always the chance of storms driving them right out of reach'.

'Without a storm, under normal sea conditions', I wondered, 'how long can you expect them to remain static?'

Whittaker, I could see, was on the point of responding.

The sharp voice of a rating turned his attention from me.

'Looks like a sub, sir'.

Whittaker bent to the screen, and whistled. 'A mighty big one, too'.

The sonar image left no doubt about the object that was approaching underwater from the northeast. Its course and speed were constant, its size remarkable.

Without hesitation, yet with the utmost sang-froid, Whittaker called up submarine-hunter aircraft from Lossiemouth.

'None of the western powers has anything like this size', he told me.

'How big is she?'

'Can't tell until she's a lot nearer, but it looks as though she could be about twice the size of an average attack sub'.

A submarine wanting to launch a missile at us would have no need to come anywhere within a thousand miles of the island. Approaching like this could mean only that she were to land a man. Or men.

Clearly, the man killed here a few nights ago was to be replaced. This time we should have the advantage, being able to watch him coming ashore right from the moment that he left the sub.

'Do the Chinese have a submarine of this size?' I asked.

'Not too sure. They bought a few from the Russians, but I don't believe there were any big ones among them'.

'The Typhoon was Russia's big one, wasn't it?'

'That's what we called her, but the Russian name for her was Shark. Never seen one in the metal, as it were; only intelligence pictures. I do know that she was supposed to be nearly two hundred yards long, if you can believe that'.

'Could the Chinese have copied it, or developed one of their own?'

'Could have, certainly. Though why on earth anyone would send something that big to land a man escapes me. Testing our defences, possibly'.

'And giving the crew invaluable training'.

'Of course'.

I had heard that submarines could be converted into cargo carriers by removing the torpedo tubes and of course also the space-consuming store of torpedoes themselves. The same modifications to a larger sub, it seemed to me, would provide space to carry a sizeable company of marines. I put this to Whittaker.

He compressed his lips. 'Difficult to know what to hope for. Even with all her armament, a vessel that size will still have space to be carrying a lot of men. If, on the other hand, she is unarmed, well, the number of marines potentially on board doesn't bear thinking about'.

'Can we intercept before they come close enough to land?' I wondered.

'Relying on the RAF, I'm afraid. The best weapon against a submarine is another submarine – and we don't have one anywhere near. You can thank the Government's so-called defence review for that. It did not review what we needed for defence, but how many savings could be made. Too much to ask, I suppose, for them to have been honest, and called it spending review'.

'Like Beeching with the railways, chopping off routes where trains are needed now'.

'Before my time, I'm afraid. What I can tell you is that as far as I know, the nearest submarine we have on patrol at present is in the Indian Ocean'.

'Great Scot! What about destroyers?'

'We can get one from Scapa Flow, but don't ask me for an estimated time of arrival'.

I didn't ask.

Instead, I leaped into my jeep and set her bouncing across what always had been, and still was, grazing land for goats.

I called at each of the two-man lookout posts in turn. No one had seen any disturbance on the sea that could have indicated a surfacing submarine. Nor were any approaching canoes to be detected.

I quickly found myself on a patch of grass that threatened to send the jeep either sliding backwards or toppling on to its side. I turned the vehicle so that it rested sideways across the slope, turned off the ignition and yanked on the handbrake.

As soon as I had one foot on the ground, I was all but blown right over by a wind as vicious as any I had experienced anywhere. I struggled to the high spot offering, as far as I could tell, the best view of where I thought that the submarine would come closest to land. Huddled down inside my duffel coat with hood up, I swept that area of sea through binoculars. What I really needed were night goggles, as well.

I'm not sure which birds it was – there were so many varieties on the island – but breaking in on what I believed to be my total concentration came a cacophony (yes, I think that word is justified; I mean nothing disparaging by it) a cacophony of bird voices. The creatures were alarmed, and they were spreading this alarm to their fellows. They were outraged, as was I to be when I reached the cliff top.

We speak of 'bird brains' derogatorily, and this may well most of the time be justified. All the same, it was birds who raised the alarm for us that night, and they were probably minutes ahead of our human lookouts.

VI

I RAN to the top of the cliff where the birds had risen en masse, dropped flat and peered down over the edge. As I have explained, Craigard had no chalk cliffs such as we know from the Dover area, but only walls of igneous granite.

At this point, the wall was indented with countless hollows, and these hollows were home to innumerable bird families. This was where pairs nested and raised their young, where they slept at night. Soldiers' boots were now in these homes. Grappling hooks had been fired and had taken a grip on the surface at the cliff top. Six of them, so far as I could see. From these dangled ropes, while on the ropes men using the birds' tiny ledges as toeholds were hauling themselves towards the surface where I lay in wait.

If I tell you that my first instinct was to open fire at once on the climbers, I hope you will not think me a trigger-happy thug. How dare anyone invade United Kingdom territory bearing arms? We have a thousand-year history of giving bloody noses to previous gangs who have tried this.

I was fuming and, I admit it freely, keyed up more than sufficiently to burst into violence on the instant. Even so, there was something – I don't know what or why – that kept my hand from squeezing the trigger until I had given the intruders fair warning.

I showed my head over the cliff edge, called for the men below to stay where they were, and asked them to identify themselves. For all I knew, none of them understood a word of English. All the same, I reasoned that they could not fail to recognize my scarcely welcoming tone. Equally, they must know how they themselves would receive our forces if we were to land on their home soil.

I had intended to follow my challenge with a warning shot out to sea. There was no time. I was answered with a dozen bullets zipping past my head.

I rolled away from the edge of the cliff and took a grenade in my hand. I pulled out the pin and waited for two seconds. Stretching my hand forward over the cliff edge, I let the grenade fall.

The explosion must have come about halfway between cliff top and sea level. I took a rapid look over the cliff edge, and switched on my torch. Well blooded corpses had fallen from four of the six ropes. I fired off a full automatic magazine at the men I could see waiting for their turns to begin climbing, and pulled back my head and shoulders so that once again I could not be seen from below.

If I had deceived myself about being able to stem a landing with hand grenades, I was undeceived practically on the instant. I had not considered, as I should have, that two could play at that game.

Crash! An explosion on my left sent me rolling away to my right. Crash! I had all but rolled into the centre of the next explosion. The men below the cliff had put a grenade either side of me. Of course they had. Isn't that exactly what I should have done in a situation like theirs?

I climbed to my feet. These were bigger grenades than the one I had dropped on them. They would not be tossed by a man who had his hands full climbing, but sent on their way from down at the water's edge. They could not have been thrown. To attain such a height, they must have been fired from a hand-held grenade launcher.

For the next half minute or longer, I was deaf. And also, I must admit it, a little stunned. Just when I was beginning to believe that my eardrums had gone altogether, I realized that I was after all hearing again, and that what I was hearing was an urgent scrambling. I had not destroyed the ropes dangling from the grappling hooks, and each of these was being climbed.

The Chinese, if they were Chinese, were swarming up half a dozen ropes simultaneously. I should never be able to prevent all of them from reaching the top.

I de-pinned two grenades simultaneously and lobbed them underhand down the ropes together. This cleared the field for the moments that I needed to place an unpinned grenade beneath each of the grappling irons.

The explosions of these, following closely on each other, dislodged wedges of soil and rock. Five of the grappling irons fell back, clattering as they bounced repeatedly off the rock face. Good. I could deal one by one with those coming up the remaining rope.

I gripped my automatic pistol, and fired straight into the first face that hauled itself above the summit of the cliff. The face vanished, and I fired at another that appeared almost immediately. A third and a fourth came into view, and I despatched each in the same way.

Then a third grenade crashed behind me. The blast very nearly pitched me forward over the cliff.

I stumbled, rather than raced, to the cover of my jeep. Dropping flat behind it, I took a fresh, fully loaded pistol and lay with it levelled between the wheels towards the cliff edge.

Another face appeared over the edge of the cliff. I fired, and it vanished. At once another took its place. Then another, and another.

It was extraordinary. No. More than extraordinary. It was incredible. Literally. If I had not experienced it, I should never have believed it possible. As fast as I despatched each invader, another took his place. These men showed no reluctance at all about going forward to be killed. Were they perhaps a Chinese version of Japan's Kamikaze pilots?

How many were down there, queuing up to be killed? I could not be sure that my ammunition would hold out.

It would not need to. Jardine was not the man to leave defence either to chance or to individuals. I have never seen anyone so rapid in activity nor so cool in command.

As soon as my exchange of fire and grenades had started, Jardine despatched two jeeps full of men to help me out. He set off himself along the coast with a half dozen men in one of the island's three motor boats. A second boat started directly behind Jardine's. Both boatloads were on top of the would-be invaders while these were still tackling the cliff face.

Jardine had his men on full alert. In line with conventional counter-attack thinking, he was waiting to see what sort of landing was being undertaken before making his final dispositions. It was, he thought, essential to see the invading force commit itself, so that we should know what was its objective.

I on the other hand had urged him beforehand to open his attack while invaders were at their most vulnerable, namely, while they were still on the water. I saw no virtue in waiting for an opponent to land before challenging and opening fire.

Jardine would challenge, I knew, before firing. The invaders, though, were likely to open fire at once.

Why had these men come, when their scout had failed to return or even to make contact after sending through the pictures that he had taken? And why send men ashore at all, when they could launch a rocket, perhaps to wipe out our laboratories completely and certainly to set Britain's work back many years? A Typhoon, or Shark, submarine could direct a strategic missile to Britain from underneath the Arctic ice.

Yet surely the Chinese were not entrusting this whole enterprise to the few men who would make it up a rock face? This landing, I was convinced, was no more than a feint. There had to be more. Much more. Their full assault must be mounted elsewhere.

I set the jeep leaping and bouncing over the turf in a more or less circular tour of those cliff tops overlooking places where others might have landed.

In every direction the blackness was complete. The howling wind was all but deafening.

I had covered perhaps half of my circuit when the penny dropped. What a dolt I had been! What was it that the Chinese wanted to bring ashore? It would be impractical to haul anything at all sizeable up a cliff face. Surely their main landing must come at our only beach.

I raced the jeep back downhill towards the water's edge, and switched on the beach-facing floodlights I had set up. There or rather here – they were. Two-man canoes heading towards the shoreline on a making tide. While each in turn dipped out of sight into the waves it was difficult to be certain of their number. As near as I could make it, I concluded that there were thirty canoes each carrying two men.

The rearward man in each canoe was rotating a double-ended paddle in relentless rhythm, driving the inflatable landwards. The forward man carried an automatic weapon directed over the bow.

Jardine's men maintained perfect discipline. Each had an automatic rifle trained on the forward man in one of the approaching inflatables. None fired.

I called for the canoeists to identify themselves. As on the cliff top, my answer was a swarm of bullets. Jardine's men opened up at once. Two-way automatic fire was interspersed with grenade blasts. The exchange lasted probably no longer than twenty seconds. Then there was silence and a sea so laden with bodies that it reminded me of pictures of lumberjacks' log jams. Once again I was struck by the contrast with what I had seen in the cinema. Gun battles on screen are always spun out to an absurd length. Exchanges of fire in real life are brief.

I hopped into my jeep, and set off to return to the scene of the cliff top shootings. Halfway there, I was forced by undulations in the ground to turn eastwards to where I found myself looking directly out to sea.

A stirring in the water, and despite the opaqueness of the night I had no difficulty in making out what was happening. Amid a swirl of sea, the conning tower of a submarine was emerging.

As I learned later, this was a vessel capable of firing off two dozen intercontinental ballistic missiles. What it did once it had broken the surface of the Atlantic was to open up with small automatic cannon. Our clifftop defenders were first to be hit, then our two launches. Jardine's vessel disappeared at once. Its companion flew into pieces just as I became aware of the sound of Tornado aircraft.

The RAF boys wasted no time. Two small missiles flew down to strike the submarine at the base of its conning tower, then two more, from a second aircraft, plunged through the upper skin of the vessel. A detonation nearer to hand told me that the barrel of Craigard's lone AA gun had been depressed to fire from its hillside emplacement directly at the submarine. There was an explosion on the sea suggestive of the destruction of an ammunition store, and when the smoke cleared there was no more to be seen of the submersible giant.

We had lost a lot of men, though Jardine and a half dozen others from the two motor boats had survived their sinking.

With the loss of their submarine, the invaders had no means of escape. Our men, both on cliff top and at the beach, called in vain for the raiders to surrender. As before, the answer was a storm of fire.

We did not want to kill all of the intruders. We needed some whom we could interrogate, so that we could understand the whole hare-brained exercise.

Yet we were compelled not to cease firing until all invaders at the beach were dead. Every raider fought until he was killed. What we did not know was that when a man ran out of ammunition, he leaped into the water and charged towards our men with weapon still directed forward. Only once we recovered the dead did we discover how many had run into our fire with magazines empty. It had been less a gun battle than mass suicide.

For a stretch of some thirty yards out from the beach, the sea bore up the bodies of men who had refused to bow before our fire. The remains of a number of inflatable canoes, nearly all torn to pieces, drifted between them. We could walk from one headland of the beach to another, stepping all the way from body to body – or so it seemed.

Of the cliff-scaling party, only four were still alive, among them one officer. We were able to lay our hands on these four only because each was so badly wounded as to be incapable of further activity.

So pressing was our need for intelligence that Jardine, himself with wounds to arm and back, asked Captain Naismith and his medical orderlies to treat the captured wounded officer before any of our own boys.

It had been a particularly dark night, and the day that followed came in, it seemed, grudgingly. The sun, when we first saw it, looked severely undernourished, and even by midday appeared scarcely better fed.

One after another, the helicopters came in to take away the worst of our wounded – insofar as they were fit to be transported – for treatment at Army hospitals on the mainland.

A naval team arrived, sending divers down to the wrecked submarine. These established that the vessel was completely broken in two, and that no one on board was alive. The most significant of their finds was the captain's log.

The language expert we had requested, Millie, arrived with one of the morning's helicopters. She was as petite and dainty as any Japanese girl in a 19th century engraving, and came to us with a warning. We should not, we were told, let appearances deceive us. Millie was proficient in martial arts up to one of the highest grades. Where languages were concerned, she was as expert as they came. The Service, it was rumoured, had with difficulty fended off several Foreign Office attempts to 'poach' her.

Let me at this point affirm, in case anyone should expect otherwise, that there was to be no 'romance' between Millie and myself. We had work to do together, and that was all.

Emotionally, I was still totally absorbed in Anna. And always shall be. Meeting Anna had been the greatest miracle of my life. No. Scrub that. The greatest miracle was that she said yes to me, and I still found it a cause for wonder. It was inexplicable.

I was an early riser. Most days during our years together, when I woke I would lie in bed for an extra several minutes, doing no more than gaze at Anna's face while she slept on.

In an evening, when she would snuggle up to me on the sofa, I would stroke her blonde waves, her cheek, her neck, and wonder for the nth tine what I could possibly have done to merit such bliss.

Anna had brought so much into my life: warmth, gentleness, contentment and an emotional stability the need for which I had never imagined. She had opened up my mind, too – or was it my emotions that she had lightened? Before we met, I had tended to be swift in judgement and forthright in condemning inadequacy of any kind. Once Anna had entered my life, she would counter where appropriate with a temperate reminder that human fallibility was common to all. More often than not, her words compelled me to concede that I had been hasty and lacking in compassion. From Anna I had learned to attempt an understanding of my fellows rather than judging them.

What, in turn, could I offer Anna? Unwavering devotion, beyond question. Against this, I had subjected her to the uncertainties and material insufficiencies of my life in the Service. A terrible bargain for her. Anna could have done so much better for herself. And should have done.

I did not deserve the girl, and was astonished that she did not seem to know this. One day, I always feared, the thought would come to her, and then...

Losing Anna had been the worst nightmare that I could imagine. Those imaginings had been selfish.

What did any hurt to me matter? The agony that Anna came to suffer was the unbearable, the unthinkable affliction. Watching her pain drove me into a madness that led me to dream the impossible: that I could pass on to Anna the unexpired portion of my own life, my likely term of years to come. Then I should joyfully have leaped into my grave to allow Anna her natural span of time.

In short, I was as much in love with Anna at the end as on the day of our wedding. If anything, even more in love with her.

If I had been asked about my dearest wish I should surely have said that it was to die in Anna's arms. A second later I would retract this statement, knowing that such a wish would be entirely selfish, an unfair and intolerable imposition for her.

I still dreamed of Anna at night, thought about her in every quiet moment during the day. Anna had been part of me, would always be a part. I had been devoted to Anna since that first sighting at the Lehrter railway station in Berlin. I should go to my grave devoted to her.

Millie was charming, but I was immune.

The brigadier put Millie through the usual Official Secrets routine but was unable to let her loose on the submarine captain's log. By order of the MoD, this had been despatched to Whitehall before Millie arrived.

As it happened, we did not need Millie to identify the invaders. We already knew who they were. They were not Chinese after all.

VII

JARDINE's men had faced attacks on two fronts, and had not only fought off the invaders, but shown unruffled efficiency in action. Jardine himself was unperturbed by his own wounds, and concerned only for the families of the men he had lost.

At the beach, only two of our soldiers had been hit. They had minor bullet wounds. Jardine's losses were on the cliff top and among those who had sailed with him in the two motor boats.

Here I should state that the numbers of both our own losses and those of the invader remain classified secrets. In the early stages of writing down this narrative, I received a visit from two Army officers of field rank (that is, major and above). They arrived in full uniform and served me with a D-notice on this topic, a ban on revealing any of the figures concerning losses.

All that I may say is that the reader is correct in inferring UK losses to have been but a miniscule fraction of the invader's figures.

The raiders had lost the entire crew of their submarine, every man of the sixty who had attempted a landing at the beach, and all but four of those tackling the cliff ascent.

To a man, the landing parties had continued to press forward regardless of the automatic fire that was concentrated on them from more than a hundred weapons. Both those on the sea and those scaling the cliff were exposed to the defending forces without a shred of cover. They refused all appeals to cease fire, continuing until the last man was dead.

Their willingness to die had confounded everyone on the island. This was a dimension to fire fights quite unknown to European forces.

Recovering bodies from the water took all of the rest of the night, and we were still not certain that we had all from the submarine. The vessel was so large, with so many compartments, that some crew members were certain to have been trapped at their stations and, of course, to be there still.

One of Jardine's subalterns took charge of working parties engaged in gathering our dead and laying them out in one of the utility buildings. The invaders' dead were placed in ranks in the open, on soft young turf.

An officer's cap floating with other debris from the submarine was one of the first items recovered. I knew the badge at once. It was that of the North Korean Navy.

Had this cap been the only North Korean item picked up, I should have thought that its wearer had been an observer invited on board for a mission of the Chinese or Russian navy. Yet uniforms of the many dead confirmed within a few minutes that the whole affair was North Korean. Here was a navy that we had all believed had only a few out of date ships. The giant vessel sent on this raid must just about have bankrupted the country, whether it had been built there or bought from the Russians or Chinese.

Now that Iraq had lost that distinction, North Korea had the world's fourth largest army. Her air force had effective Russian attack aircraft, but her navy had always been the poor relation of the country's forces. Until now, North Korea had lacked the resources even to conduct joint exercises with her two fleets, one stationed on the west coast and the other on the east flank of the peninsula.

What had prompted this dramatic swing in priorities? It looked as though the country's leaders had realized that their navy was the means of projecting the power to which they aspired. That power, though, was illusory – even more so now that the submarine was lost.

Whom had North Korea wanted to threaten or impress with a super-sub? Surely only South Korea or Japan. In any case, China held the whip hand in the region. North Korea was dependent on the good will of Beijing, particularly since the collapse of Communism elsewhere meant that aid from Russia was throttled right back.

China, I felt sure, would not like to see North Korea disturbing the precarious power balance in the Northern and Western Pacific. Nor would Britain be fair game for a spot of sabre-rattling. With the Hong Kong question solved, there were no significant issues outstanding between China and the UK.

Nor were there between North Korea and the UK. So what had been the purpose of the raid?

We had four wounded prisoners. Unquestionably, these would be as careless of their lives as their now dead comrades had been. Interrogation was liable to be fruitless.

A dozen of the dead had been carrying explosive charges. It looked as though they had intended to destroy our installations. Yet it had been a somewhat elaborate raid for doing something that a handful of men could have executed efficiently.

Our Royal Navy divers were quick workers. While we were still struggling to sort out our dead, they reported with two laptops from the submarine.

'How long to dry them out without damage?' was the only question on my mind. I had heard of data from mobile phones and even from tape recorders being recovered after the devices had spent as much as a year under water.

About the laptops our boffins were sanguine. 'If they are not damaged beyond use already, they should be usable in twenty four hours'.

Now came one of those curious contradictions which bedevil life in government service. Having prevented our looking at the submarine captain's log by demanding its immediate despatch to the MoD, Whitehall paradoxically made no objection to our hanging on to the two captured laptops. Our technicians were left to recover all the data that had ever been on them, allowing Millie to settle down into a marathon of translation.

'That log should in any case have gone to the Admiralty', Whittaker complained, 'not to the MoD'.

'It's a Foreign Office matter, anyhow', put in cool, clear-headed Jardine. I can't think of any way of looking at what's happened except as an act of war.

That means that everything will have to go to the Foreign Office'.

Brigadier Dickson kept all expression out of his face. 'Who fired first?'

There was no denying that on our side I had opened proceedings with my grenade. This, however, was only in response to a fusillade from below. 'Naturally', I stressed, 'I called first for them to identify themselves and to justify their arrival. Their answer was an opening round of fire. I consider the surreptitious landing of armed men to be an act of war on the part of the government that sends them. If they cannot or do not explain themselves when called upon to do so, we have no alternative but to open fire in defence'.

'No one will deny that', confirmed the brigadier, 'but the Government will need everything – *everything* – recorded in minutest detail. There are some people who would like to see every single expended round of ammunition accounted for, you can be sure. I think that we should at least try to have your full reports printed out ready for handing to our visitors as soon as these arrive with the first helicopter that comes in this morning. You had better go now and start compiling them'. From a drawer beside his knee the brigadier lifted a green bottle bearing the unmistakable label of one of the Islay distilleries. 'First, though, something to counteract the night air. You've earned it'.

Three tumblers had appeared on his desk, and the brigadier poured us each a double. I could never take whisky now without thinking of Anna and her 'blunt instrument'. This association, however, had in no way diminished my taste for the liquid panacea.

Brigadier Dickson, too, I realized as Jardine and I left him, would need to write his own report for the War House and the FO. And what about Whittaker? He was obviously going to be called on to explain his action in calling up an air strike from Lossiemouth.

'I'm going to print out three copies of my report', I told Jardine. 'One for the Army – that is, the brigadier – one for my own chief and one for the Foreign Office. Ten to one, though, that won't be enough. You might think about producing a spare copy or two, as well'.

'Thanks. That's a good tip'.

I could see that Jardine was anxious to visit those of his men who were wounded. He also needed his own wounds to be treated, though he disregarded these. In view of the brigadier's imperative, he despatched a subaltern to collect the data concerning all casualties, on both sides, then settled himself in his office to write.

In my own quarters was an Army laptop. As soon as I began setting down my report on it, I felt suddenly at home. For most of my adult life, until I had resigned to look after Anna, I had been used to writing report after report. This was a daily chore that I had chiefly found irksome, but now, I suppose because it was so familiar, I found the task surprisingly comfortable and welcome.

I wondered how the Tornado crews were coping with their own reports. It was natural to assume – but was this correct? – that they had taken enough film of the firing at our cliff edge to make superfluous any questioning of their prompt going into action.

I did not know it until I took my finished report to him, but the brigadier had himself joined our men defending the beach. 'Leaving aside the question of what was the invader's objective', he asked me, 'what did you think of the way he went about things?'

'Too simplistic to be worthy of modern forces', I told him. 'Entry via the beach was obviously their objective; the cliff landing was meant to divert our forces there, to leave the beach undefended – or at least weakly defended. Something like the sort of thing Frederick the Great did, only the wrong way round'.

The brigadier looked at me with what appeared to be curiosity. 'You mean that they should have feinted at the beach, and made their main landing at the cliff?'

'Certainly. There would always be too many losses at the beach. It would be better to commit only a few there, enough to draw fire from the cliff. Only for the purpose of securing a landing I mean, of course. Once the island was effectively occupied they would need to do their fetching and carrying via the beach'.

'Hm. You may or may not be right. Did anything strike you about the timing?'

'Too close together – though perhaps the noise up at the cliff misled them into thinking that we were almost completely engaged. So many grenades...'

'It's possible, certainly. Damned badly organized, the whole thing. And look at what it's cost them. Right, now you'd better try to snatch a little rest before our visitors fly in'.

Sleep would certainly be welcome, but first I was more interested in the condition of our wounded. I went to the sick bay, and was gratified to hear from Naismith that Jardine had been treated and sent to his bed – not, however, before he too had delivered a copy of his written report to the brigadier. All other casualties were being stitched, bandaged, plastered and otherwise cared for, with none in a life-threatening condition.

The wounds of our four prisoners had required more attention. All, patched and clothed in hospital gowns, were being kept under guard in a barrack room.

Satisfied, I went to bed. Sleep did not come. After an hour and a half of threshing about uselessly, I gave up, threw the bedclothes to one side, sprang to my feet, showered, shaved, dressed and went over my report again to see whether I had made any significant omissions. I knew the sort of detail that would be demanded. I was sure that, if anything, Foreign Office mandarins were likely to be even more meticulous in their expectations than the heads of my own Service. These, heaven knows, seem to take sadistic pleasure in squeezing additional but completely useless data from the most exhaustively compiled account.

In this case, I was satisfied that I had left nothing out of my narrative that anyone could reasonably expect to be included. Not that I expected any degree at all of reasonableness to be exhibited by my inquisitors, whoever they might be.

Rather than in the pointless hurdles of bureaucracy, I was far more interested in the welfare of our men. I visited the sick bay again, and was happy to see that Naismith, too, had finally taken himself off to bed. Three orderlies were in charge, with our wounded who were still there enjoying the peace of sleep.

One of the orderlies offered me a mug of coffee, and I have to say that after the activity of the night it seemed the purest nectar.

Light was still burning in the brigadier's office, and it occurred to me that the CO might very well be writing letters of condolence to the families of our dead.

I wondered what explanation was going to be given for these fatalities.

VIII

SINCE earlier I described the sea as leaden, it would not do for me to apply the same epithet to the sky that sulked over us that morning. The sea had been threatening and turgid; the sky, though dressed to match, a meaningless canopy of reluctance and torpor.

The night's winds had died away, the Army's coffee had done me a great deal of good, and I was in no way missing my night's sleep.

Whether Brigadier Dickson had slept, I did not know. I suspected that he had not. It made no difference. The CO exhibited admirable determination to maintain parade ground smartness and to display to whatever visitors we were to receive a unit at the peak of efficiency.

The Union Flag, lowered at sunset on the previous evening, was now raised again at the edge of the parade ground, but, in honour of our dead, only to half-mast. This ceremony was attended by a bugler and a guard of honour under Jardine's command.

In the workshops, men were putting together coffins for the transportation of our dead back to the mainland. Meanwhile, the invader's dead, lying as they had been placed, in rows under the sky, had been covered with tarpaulins pegged into the soil.

We did not wait long before the familiar engine drones emerged from that tedious sky. They brought with them not one, but three helicopters, flying very high.

Jardine had organized a guard of honour – six men with rifles at the slope. He and the brigadier wore swords.

One after another, the helicopters described a half circle over the island, lost height rapidly and settled without hesitation. Engines stopped, rotors relaxed into a halt, doors slid open. From the first machine clambered a posse of obvious civil servants. MoD or Foreign Office? Two or three of them looked as though they were relieved to have ground under their feet again. They were followed by three RAF officers, one evidently of high rank.

The second machine brought Army brass, the third a delegation from the Admiralty, accompanied by the deputy chief and a departmental head from my own service.

As each group was decanted, Jardine brought his men to the 'present arms' salute. The brigadier stepped forward to welcome the visitors, and Jardine led them past his guard of honour. All then trooped into the briefing room used for training lectures.

Jardine had been busy. Copies of his report, mine and that from Whittaker had been distributed to every seat. A tea urn and coffee machines were on a table, with orderlies on hand to fulfil wishes. The brigadier spoke.

'Gentlemen, I think it best for you first to take your seats and read the reports that are before you. Once you are familiar with the outline of events, we can have you put your questions to the authors. Refreshment is available. Orderlies will come round to serve you. You will find the usual facilities through that door'.

As each man read, notebooks and pens appeared. On the whole, ministry men scribbled fiercely, and with alarmed expressions. Service personnel, I noticed, showing no feeling, contented themselves with terse notes.

The two men from my own service did not look towards me. They remained intent on the reports, making sporadic notes in the margins.

Once everyone had worked his way through the reports, the brigadier took his seat at the centre of the dais, flanked by a General Staff colonel, a vice-admiral and the senior of the three RAF officers. These were in full uniform. Also on the dais were the deputy chief of my own service and a civilian whom I took to be a highly placed figure from the Foreign Office.

Jardine, Lieutenant-Commander Whittaker, the two junior RAF men and I were to sit at a table below the dais, placed to one side so as to face across the room. The assembly, I thought, began to look like a court martial, with the five of us as the accused.

Opposite us, we faced another table. Recognizable on it were items from the submarine – including the officer's cap – and some weapons from the storming troops. On the floor in front of the table was the inflatable canoe that I had located in the water. These, then, were the exhibits for the prosecution. Millie, the translator, sat behind this table. The two laptops from the submarine were open before her.

A large scale coloured map of the island, complete with pointer, was on an easel alongside our table.

It was clearly going to be difficult to maintain any sort of logical sequence for questions from so many individuals. I wondered whether the brigadier might not ask for questions to be written down for submission.

'I think it best', he announced, 'if we allow the gentlemen from the Foreign Office to put their questions first, then take those from the armed services in order of the forces' seniority – by which I mean of course Royal Navy first'.

A man rose whose face I recognized. He was evidently a senior man from the Foreign Office delegation, and he had represented the FO at Anna's funeral. He had written me a formulaic letter of condolence, and I remembered that his name was Desmond Anthony Martin Northall. From the attitude he displayed now, I was to reflect that his names could scarcely have yielded a more appropriate acronym.

'The man Greig admits to opening the firing', Northall began. 'Does he realize what consequences this is likely to have for Britain's relations not just with North Korea, but also with China, and possibly with Russia, too?

I was on the point of rising to answer with some heat, when the brigadier cut in to my defence. 'Greig, sir, has made it quite clear that the invaders fired first. Greig challenged them to identify themselves and state the purpose of their landing. In reply he was fired at by several men. It was only then that he opened defensive fire with a hand grenade'.

Northall was not satisfied. 'That is indeed what Greig says in his report. Major...' Northall lifted a second report and consulted it '...Jardine's report is, I take it, accurate?'

Jardine spoke for himself. 'It is, sir, in every particular'.

'Yet Major Jardine states that the first he heard of firing was the detonation of a grenade, which Greig later admitted to have been one that he had dropped onto men endeavouring to scale a cliff'.

Jardine was on his feet. 'Yes, sir. That was the first detonation that I heard'.

'You were yourself where, Major?

'A matter of some twenty five or thirty yards inland from the beach, with the men I had placed there to await any possible landing'.

'So, if I read the map correctly, you were little more than half a mile – let us be generous, and say a thousand yards – from the spot where Greig opened his attack with a grenade, and where he claims previously to have come under rifle fire?'

'Around a thousand yards, I should say without measuring it, sir, yes'.

'Yet the first that you heard of any fire fight was the detonation of the grenade with which Greig admits that he opened the encounter?'

'It was the first that I heard, yes, sir, but the wind that night was so strong that I should not have expected to hear rifle shots over such a distance, particularly since the men who fired them...'

'Whom Greig alleges fired them'.

Jardine was needled. 'If Greig says that they fired them, I am certain, sir, that that was so. As I was saying, I should not have expected to hear rifle shots discharged a thousand yards away, from the base of a cliff some two hundred and fifty feet high – not with that wind'.

'Indeed?' Northall was determined to pursue this point. He demanded weather records for the previous twenty four hours, and was visibly disappointed to learn that the midnight wind had been the strongest recorded on the island for a matter of nearly twenty one months. 'But a rifle shot is sharp', he persisted, 'surely it would penetrate for a thousand yards or so, despite the wind'. This was not a question. Northall had made up his mind, and that was that.

'Sir', responded Jardine, 'as it happens I only just heard the grenade detonation. That came across as rather muffled. What one heard principally was the wind. Rifle shots obviously had no chance of coming through'.

'For the discharge of rifle shots from down below the cliff you have only Greig's word, is that not so, Major?'

'Yes'.

That the men who landed had been bearing loaded weapons, had not been invited by Her Majesty's Government, had given no notice of arrival and had landed by stealth were factors that Brigadier Dickson put to Northall with considerable earnestness.

'All that you say, Brigadier', Northall countered, 'is no doubt sufficient reason for your own men and for all the members of our fighting services to react with armed force to an uninvited landing by foreign troops – after appropriate challenges and warnings first, of course. None of these circumstances can, however, justify Greig's action. Greig is not a serviceman in any of Her Majesty's armed forces. It is clear that he seized the opportunity to start his own personal war against North Korea, just as his late wife waged her own against the leadership of the Soviet Union. Greig evidently has no conception of the efforts that Her Majesty's Government was forced to make, and the concessions that we were compelled to agree, after he had made public the facts of that earlier private war. Now he has started all over again with this latest chapter in his one-man crusade against Communism. He must realize that this time, should Pyongyang demand his extradition, which she is thoroughly entitled to do, he need not expect HMG necessarily to oppose this'.

I knew that this was nonsense, that the United Kingdom had no extradition treaty with North Korea. Knew also that Northall would be fully aware of this.

Nonetheless, because of his references to Anna I might have sprung up and flown at Northall, had the disciplined Jardine not restrained me with a hand on my arm.

'I think', said the Brigadier, 'that we should leave the question of possible diplomatic embarrassments to those who deal with these things, and proceed with examination of what actually took place here during the night. Perhaps', turning to the admiral at his side, 'you would like to open the questions'.

IX

'**R**ATHER than question', began the vice-admiral, 'I should like to begin by praising all concerned in defeating this extraordinary attempt to invade British soil. A remarkable example, I must say, of inter-service cooperation – even more remarkable, and probably unique, for a submarine to be sunk by an anti-aircraft gun. With assistance from the Royal Air Force, naturally'.

This produced some clapping and light laughter. My impression was that there was relief in that laughter. Northall's attacks had not gone down well with many of those present.

'Lieutenant-Commander Whittaker', resumed the admiral, 'can you give an estimate at what distance from your sonar station the hostile submarine was first detected?'

'Very roughly only, sir, but I think it must have been about four miles'.

'And you were in no doubt from that moment that it was a submarine?'

'No doubt at all, sir'.

'Her size did not cause you any doubt?'

'It caused me surprise, sir. My first thought was that it must be a Russian Typhoon, probing our defences'.

'Just trying it on, you mean? You did not suspect any hostile action beyond stealthy reconnaissance of our defences?'

'No, sir'.

'And you assumed that she was Russian?'

'Russia was so far as I knew the only country with a submarine of that size, sir'.

'Quite so. And you called for submarine-hunter aircraft from RAF Lossiemouth for what purpose?'

'In the expectation that they could fly low over the intruder in our waters and frighten her off – particularly if she were to surface. In the way that our fighters escort aerial intruders out of our air space'.

'Indeed. You had detected a foreign submarine about four miles from this island, and heading this way. Here was a clear intrusion into UK territorial waters. Your actions, Lieutenant-Commander, were entirely correct'.

'Thank you, sir'.

'Now, the island had an intruder, a solitary man, on the night before this episode. Was his approach, or the approach of any vessel, detected then on your sonar equipment?'

'No, sir'.

'Why do you think that was, Lieutenant-Commander?'

'Whatever ship brought him must have approached the island on our blind side – that is, where we have no sonar equipment. He evidently paddled ashore in an inflatable canoe. Mr Greig located that canoe, deflated, hidden under water near the beach. It is available for your inspection, sir, right here on the floor'.

'And the purpose of that solitary visitor's arrival? I take it that you can offer an explanation deductively?'

'Perhaps, sir', began Jardine, 'I should answer this. Lieutenant-Commander Whittaker has not seen these photographs'. Jardine had a briefcase on the floor beside his chair. From it he took the visitor's camera and a folder containing eight by ten inch enlargements of the photographs that had been found on it. He handed both items to an orderly, who passed them up to the admiral. 'You will see, sir', Jardine continued, 'that together these photographs provide a complete picture of all the installations on this island. The purpose of that one-man visit was clearly reconnaissance'.

'But if the man were killed, and you had his camera, his reconnaissance mission will not have done his comrades much good, will it? Yet they came anyway, did they not?'

'If I might explain, sir. A memory card in this camera – bearing all the photographs taken – can be removed and placed into a slot in a mobile telephone. The photographs can then be transmitted. When this man was shot, the card was in the telephone, not in the camera'.

'So that it is reasonable to assume that the man had either already transmitted the photographs or was about to do so?'

'Certainly. I should explain that the mobile telephone in question has only a short range. This puzzled us at first. However, Royal Navy divers have now provided us with an explanation. On board the submarine they found a drone – a pilotless flying machine controlled from the submarine. This drone could be released whenever the submarine surfaced. It would take only a matter of a minute for the drone to receive incoming messages – in this case, all of the pictures taken here. The drone would then return to the vessel, and be stowed aboard before the submarine re-submerged. I believe we can take it, sir, that thanks to these photographs all members of the landing party – or parties – were well briefed on the complete layout here on the island'.

The admiral was content. 'Thank you, Major. My other queries concern the nature of the submarine, and these can be answered only once our men have completed a minute inspection'.

The admiral gave a light nod towards the brigadier, who had some key questions for Jardine. 'Major Jardine, I was with you at the beach, and am familiar with events in practically all of their details. For the benefit, however, of our civilian guests, I should like you to elaborate on what is in your report concerning the fact that those who landed or were attempting a landing at the beach were all killed'.

'As you saw for yourself, sir', Jardine confirmed, 'every man of the beach landing party conducted himself as though insusceptible to wounds. All carried on storming towards us, even after they had clearly been hit several times. They continued with their charge, on foot or still in canoes, until a fatal wound was inflicted'.

'But how can you tell us this? You were not at the beach all the time, were you, Major?' The voice was that of Northall.

'Part way through this action I left with a small party in a motor boat to give assistance to Mr Greig, who was trying to fend off the cliff landing entirely on his own'.

'So you cannot really testify as to what took place at the beach to result in the deaths of all those men? You cannot testify from your own certain knowledge – I mean, from what you yourself actually saw and heard?'

'No, sir, I cannot'.

'Some members of what you call the landing party at the beach were still alive when you left the scene in a motor boat?'

'There was still firing taking place, so naturally I assume that some men were still alive'.

'You assume. Thank you, Major'.

Brigadier Dickson's voice was icy. 'I was present, *Mr* Northall, until the conclusion of the action, and can assure you that what Major Jardine has committed to his report is nothing but the sheer unadulterated truth. Every man of the landing party, without exception, continued to charge or paddle furiously towards our men until not one of them was left alive. Even when they had emptied their magazines, they charged with empty rifles. I am aware that this is something unknown in the wars of European nations, but it happened. The single man who landed earlier to conduct photographic reconnaissance fought to the death in exactly the same way'.

'Do we know yet what was the object of this raid? I suppose I must call it a raid, not just a landing'. The questioner wore civilian clothes, but sat with a group separated from Northall. I took it therefore that he was from the MoD or the Admiralty.

'We do not yet know', admitted the brigadier. 'I suggest that we first take a look at the two scenes of action – the beach and the cliff – so as to give everyone a better appreciation of the events described. Then we shall gather for lunch, which in view of our numbers we shall have to take in the Other Ranks' dining hall. You will understand that in such a small establishment as this our officers' mess is regrettably inadequate'.

I myself drove a first party of VIPs (no Foreign Office men among them, I am thankful to say) to the cliff top where scars of the foiled landing were plentiful. The grenades both detonated by me and fired at me had ripped away chunks of soil and left black patches on the exposed rock. The scene looked worse, frankly, than I had expected. Had Jardine and his boatloads not arrived when they did, I was sure that I could not have held off every attempt by the invader to reach the top.

The remainder of the visiting party arrived in groups of four or five. The FO contingent looked at the damaged ground, and made no comment.

Having lost to fire from the submarine both boats that Jardine had used, we had only one left. All the VIPs were taken in relays to survey the cliff base where we had lost our own men. All having visited the cliff top, I was myself free to join the last of these parties. Looking up from sea level to the cliff top, I was able to appreciate how bold was the manoeuvre that the North Koreans had attempted.

X

BEFORE we gathered to go in for lunch, I called at the sick bay to ask Naismith how our wounded were coming along. A secondary reason for this visit – let me be frank – was that it kept me out of the way of the Foreign Office lot. Thrown in with them, I did not trust myself not to say something inflammatory.

In his small operating theatre-cum-autopsy-laboratory, I found Naismith performing a post mortem examination on one of the invader dead. It was, he told me, eyes gleaming, the second he had done that morning.

Naismith's excitement was unmistakeable. 'Haven't autopsied any of our own dead yet', he confessed, 'but I really had to know about these chaps'. This was a man bursting to share his discoveries. 'Would you believe it? Both these two have lesions to the amygdala, like the first chap'.

An awareness stirred somewhere in my brain. 'But not born with them?'

'Emphatically not. Look at this'. Naismith showed me a scar on the neck, behind and a little lower than the left ear. 'This is where they went in. A small excision in the amygdala, and you have a man oblivious to danger'.

Now the penny dropped. A whole company impervious to danger!

'Are you going to look at them all?' I asked.

'Might not need to go inside. Just seeing the scar on the neck will tell me'.

Of course, they would all have that scar.

There were two big questions about this episode. Why had the invaders all run straight into death like lemmings, and why had they been sent?

At least we now knew the answer to the first. This was a new kind of enemy that we should have to face.

'You'll have to come and tell our VIPs', I told the MO. 'There seems to be an idea that we made it all up and simply slaughtered the invader for the fun of it. Can you do a quick check on as many as possible of their dead – quickly enough to come and tell your tale in the briefing room before our visitors fly off again? I've no doubt that most of them will want to get away before dark'.

'Oh, I can have a look at them all fairly rapidly. Just send an orderly for me when you're ready'.

I went in search of Jardine. Outside the briefing room, the brigadier detached himself from a group of visitors and beckoned. 'Even now that they've had a look at the terrain for themselves', he warned, 'the FO people are still out for your blood. They seem convinced that you started things for reasons of your own. That head man of theirs, repulsive fellow, is demanding a full public inquiry. He wants your head on a plate, even thinks I should be holding you under arrest here'.

I thanked the brigadier for this warning, and was relieved to be able to speak to him alone. I gave him the gist of Naismith's findings. Naismith had shown the CO the amygdala of the first visitor, as he had shown it to me. Like myself, the brigadier and Jardine had regarded the abnormality merely as a curiosity. We were complete laymen; the oddity could mean nothing to us.

Thanks to Naismith's diligence, we now understood what we had been facing. 'We'd better hear from Naismith a.s.a.p.', said the CO. 'Tell him to bring some samples with him. Give the audience a nasty shock'.

While we were at lunch, Naismith was engaged in a quick tour of the enemy dead. All except submarine crew bore the unmistakable scar of a surgical entry wound in the same place on the left side of the neck. 'If they want me to look inside all of them, I'll do that', he told me. 'But I know what I'll find in every case'.

Of course he did. And so did I. So, too, would every single man in the briefing room once they had heard Naismith's exposition and seen the incisions to an amygdala.

Leaving the dining hall, I found myself behind Millie. 'Anything on those computers?' I asked.

'I think I've found something, but don't want to say anything to the others'.

Millie was quite right. She was employed by my Service, so her duty was to report to me. It would be my decision whether I passed on anything.

'What sort of thing?' I asked.

'The reason that they came'.

I drew Millie away from the crowd. 'Come and tell me about it'.

'It's on one of the computers, probably written by the political officer'.

Ever since the creation of the Red Army by Leon Trotsky, Communist armed forces had included political officers in every unit. These looked continually over military officers' shoulders, making sure that what the Party expected was pursued in all its rigour.

'I'd only just found it when we broke for lunch', said Millie. 'A reference to a birthday present for the Supreme Leader'.

'The birthday's soon, is it?'

'In two weeks'.

'Any mention what the present was to be?'

'Not sure yet. I'll have to work my way through it, but if I understand another comment correctly it looks as though they wanted to kidnap your scientists'.

XI

S O now we knew. Britain's top boffins. A birthday present for the Supreme Leader. I hoped they realized that a boffin is for life, not just for birthdays.

Yet how had they planned to take everyone out to the submarine? In those canoes? Were they after equipment, too? Unlikely. Yes, there was plenty of room on board such a leviathan, but carrying machines out to it would be scarcely practical. The explosives that some of the men had carried were surely meant to destroy everything that the abducted boffins would leave behind.

On the other hand, these fellows obviously had no limits to their imaginative audacity. From now on, we should be surprised at nothing undertaken by North Korea.

Naismith carried out yet another autopsy before appearing in the briefing room. How often does one encounter an expert who knows his subject backwards but is hopeless at communicating it to others. Naismith turned out to be one of those exceptional types with an inborn capacity for making the esoteric readily lucid.

That he fascinated his audience was a matter for gratification. Serviceman and civilian alike listened to Naismith's explanations, followed his blackboard diagrams and examined his amygdala samples, complete with lesions, in rapt silence. At the close, his listeners broke into spontaneous applause.

There was, I felt, relief all round. No one had liked the business of having to slaughter every opponent except for only those four who were so wounded as to be unable to continue the fight.

Naismith's explanation would ease many a mind.

'If this is to be the army of the future', the brigadier summarized, 'I can see early recourse to weapons of mass destruction. There's not going to be much demand for old fashioned battlefield fire fights'.

'Would we want to operate on our own men like that, though?' The questioner, in civilian clothes, was from the MoD.

'And would we be able to afford it?' wondered another. 'What on earth must such operations cost?'

'Another point', put in an Admiralty officer. 'The effects of this operation would stay with the individual for life. Would he be safe in the community, once his military service was finished?'

'It doesn't look', concluded the brigadier, 'as though our visitors were safe even during their military service. They were presumably their country's élite troops, and they threw everything away rather than make sure that sufficient numbers of them survived to complete their mission'.

'And that mission was? Do we yet know?' This was the General Staff colonel.

'As it happens, I believe that we do', I told him. During Naismith's exposition, Millie had been conducting a concentrated search of one of the submarine's laptops and making notes. From her expression of satisfaction, I was confident that she could confirm and amplify the hint that she had discovered earlier.

I nodded to Millie, and she rose. 'The object of the mission was to capture all the scientists here and take them back to work for North Korea'.

'Good lord!'

'I don't believe it'.

'Well, I'm...'

Mixed in with these expressions of wonder were the unmistakable intake of breath and one or two subdued whistles.

'It is all on this one laptop', Millie explained. 'The idea was to arrive home with the scientists in time to make a surprise birthday present of them to the Supreme Leader'.

'Confident, were they', asked the brigadier, 'that they could make them work for him?'

'The Russians made German scientists work for them', someone pointed out.

'The Russians were occupying the land where the scientists' families lived', I objected. 'In effect, they had the families as hostages. That made sure that the scientists did as they were told'.

'You're right', acknowledged the brigadier. 'North Korea could not put that kind of pressure onto our men'.

Nonetheless, both he and I knew that a threat against the individual himself would in most cases be sufficient to secure cooperation. So too, I imagined, were most of the people in the room aware of this.

'And this was to be a surprise gift, you say?' It was an RAF man who wanted clarification.

'Oh yes. That's quite clear. The whole enterprise was undertaken on the initiative of top army and navy men. It had nobody's authorization, and was as secret to Pyongyang as it was to us'.

'An individual initiative, and it cost them that submarine', mused the admiral. 'That'll have repercussions. Since they failed so miserably, what likelihood is there of a repeat attempt, I wonder?'

'None for a very long time, if ever, I should imagine'. The brigadier sounded confident. 'They have lost more than their men, who presumably formed an élite unit. As you say, they have lost that submarine, and what that cost them I daren't think. I'm no financial expert, goodness knows, but I'd be willing to bet that they will not recover from that loss for a few decades yet'.

'And meanwhile' – Northall would not let the subject go – 'we shall have the dickens of a job smoothing things over with Pyongyang'.

'And there were we thinking that it was Pyongyang who would have to try to smooth things over with us'. The brigadier had a neat delivery for his sarcasm. I noticed that I was not the only one struggling to suppress a smirk.

Northall was doubtful. 'I don't believe this nonsense for a second. No disrespect to our scientists, but why go for them instead of for the Americans? The Americans must be way ahead of us in many fields'.

'In laser weapons, certainly, but their installations are well inland, not somewhere that a commando force can raid easily. And as for abducting people... No, a coastal installation is what they needed, and Craigard is an obvious target: easy to reach, easy to land here'.

'Do we know by what route they made their way here?' It was an MoD man, speaking for the first time.

'Oh, that's easy', answered the admiral. 'A straight run under the Arctic ice cap. Nothing simpler'.

Things went on like this until the gathering ran out of questions.

It was no surprise that Northall and the rest of the Foreign Office delegation were the first to leave. 'We'll see what a full public inquiry will reveal', were Northall's words to the brigadier as they parted.

XII

WINNER in all of this was indisputably the Admiralty. The Royal Navy now had a Russian Typhoon in its hands, to examine at leisure. Admittedly, she was in two pieces, but lay in such relatively shallow water that there would be no difficulty in recovering any of her equipment for laboratory analysis. Navigation charts would be amended to keep maritime traffic away from the site of the wreck. This would be marked as a maritime grave until such time as we might be satisfied to have recovered all bodies.

There was gratification for the Army, and in particular for the anti-aircraft gun crew. Craigard's defenders had proved themselves against the toughest imaginable individual attackers. For them, the experience had proved invaluable training. The anti-aircraft gunners were cock-a-hoop, regretting only that their achievement could be given no publicity.

The RAF could chalk up a satisfying success. Its pilots had achieved swift interception, and their attack had proved the effectiveness of its small air-launched missiles.

And my own Service? I really cannot say that I had done very much at all. Recognizing what everyone else had achieved, I felt very much as though I had been a mere spectator. We knew who were our attackers, and we knew what their purpose had been. This, though, was due not to me, but to our translator, Millie.

Northall, I learned very soon, had let my chief know of his displeasure at my having been re-employed. He made his protest in such a way as to suggest that he was expressing an official Foreign Office view.

I do not doubt that the heads of my service did indeed regret pulling me from retirement for this mission. They must have wished that they had sent anyone but me. At the outset, though, there had been no indication of anything bigger than the unexplained appearance of a single man on the island. No one could have foreseen the actions that were to develop.

Whatever Headquarters' views about my part, my chiefs, I learned, defended me with some vigour against Northall's allegations. They were encouraged by Brigadier Dickson, who had apparently reacted to my critic by unleashing a storm of praise for my actions. In his eyes, he asserted, I had done exactly the right thing. As CO on Craigard he would not have had things any other way.

Northall's attempt to secure a wider inquiry into the events on Craigard found no support and was abandoned more or less at once. Recording machines had run throughout the question-and-answer sessions that the brigadier had organized, and transcripts had been sent to all parties concerned. That impromptu briefing was found to have covered the ground adequately. That at least was the official story. More likely was that no one wanted to take it further because of the need for secrecy. Beyond those few who already knew of it, the raid remained undisclosed.

I was sorry to leave Craigard. In particular I regretted having to part from Major Jardine. In very few days I had learned to admire and grown to respect Jardine. He was the coolest man under pressure that I have ever met, organizing his troops with remarkable serenity. All had total confidence in him, and it was apparent that here was a company of men who really would have followed their CO anywhere.

Jardine was exactly the sort of commander for whom I should have wished, had I become a soldier rather than what I did become.

I returned to Argyll with a conviction that I should never again be called back into service, and also with regrets that I had not done more in my life. It was too late now to make up for the years that I had spent in run-of-the-mill intelligence work, too late to switch into an occupation that would give me the thrills I had found on that cliff top with one invader's face after another popping into sight.

I had to be honest with myself. I had really enjoyed the exchange of fire, had felt more alive during it than at any time since three of us managed to abduct the Soviet agent we called Dolores. That was action. Though it had cost me a bullet in the back, I was so keyed up, had the adrenaline flowing so generously, that I felt nothing but excitement and triumph.

Three weeks at home now proved to be as much as I could stand. My mind began to wander in search of fresh pursuits. Flying, for instance. It was about time that I had myself taught to fly.

I was saved before the end of the fourth week. Would I care to return to Craigard for an indefinite period?

Two days later I was there. So already was Millie, who had stayed on to act as interpreter for the wounded prisoners. As part of the secrecy precautions, it had been decided to keep the men on Craigard. One of them had lost a hand – to a grenade of mine, I believe. A second had received a bullet through the lung, a third several shots through an upper arm and shoulder. The sole officer to survive – a young lieutenant – had abdominal wounds that should have been fatal, and normally would have been. Naismith's rapid intervention had saved this man's life when he was on the point of slipping away.

Millie had been at Naismith's side throughout the MO's treatment of all four men. She accompanied him and the medical orderlies on each of their daily visits for examination, change of dressing and so on. For historical reasons, there was no shortage of Korean antipathy towards the Japanese, who had ruled Korea until the end of the Second World War. Nonetheless, according to Naismith, the sight of such a pretty girl as Millie had helped the men recover 'faster than all my attentions'.

This was no surprise. Millie was indeed rather more than pretty; she radiated loveliness. The daily sight of such a girl at Naismith's side must have been a tonic of extraordinary power. This I was able to recognize and to understand, even though myself being insusceptible to her charms.

I arrived on the island in time to see the finishing touches being put to a small brick building constructed in typical MoD style, but at the farther end of the island from the Army's establishment. From here, all other buildings were out of sight. This new structure was to house the four prisoners, once all had recovered fully from their wounds. The building included a common recreation room and dining quarters where as nearly as possible a Korean diet would be served, cooked by a Chinese chef. The men were to be provided with Korean books, along with concealed voice-activated microphones, built into every room, enabling all their conversations to be recorded.

Whenever microphones and wiring are planted in an existing structure, there is always a risk of discovery. By implanting microphones from scratch when erecting a new building, this risk can be very nearly eliminated.

On Craigard, microphones were, so to speak, installed first, and walls built round them.

Millie and I accompanied the prisoners when they were moved into their new accommodation. We used two jeeps, with Millie as interpreter. My concern was whether the prisoners would obey instructions to climb into the jeeps and, at the other end, to go in through the doors we indicated. If these men had no fear – and we knew that this was the case – what use was an order backed by an armed guard?

In the event, we had no trouble. We saw four men installed in four rooms, and guards established in an adjoining guardroom. Back in our own accommodation in the officers' quarters, Millie settled down to monitor and translate the prisoners' conversations via a radio link. I waited to see what intelligence these might yield.

XIII

THERE was no doubt in my mind that North Korea's treatment of its soldiers, inexorably turning every assignment into a suicide mission, was proof that the Nazi gene was alive and well and living in Pyongyang.

Would we, I wondered, operate on the brains of our own forces in the same way? Could we develop the same level of contemptuous disdain for our men?

If we had ever considered it, the outcome of the North Korean raid must surely have made the folly of such a course unmistakable. Where there is no fear, there is correspondingly no thought of alternative moves to avoid disaster and to ensure success.

How many of their men had the North Koreans operated on before finding the right lesions to inflict on the amygdala for achieving the desired effect? What had been the human cost to an experiment and programme of this sort? Did anyone in the government or the army care?

I was reminded of an old Chinese saying: One does not use good iron for nails. One does not use good men as soldiers. This indicates an attitude dismissing even one's own fighting men as worthless and readily dispensable. Yet even Hitler, I reflected, had been so shocked by the losses among his paratroopers during the assault on Crete that he forbade any further paratroop operations for the rest of the war. He also refused to permit suicide flyers on the Japanese Kamikaze model, despite the fact that a ready list of suicide volunteers was placed before him. We were, it appeared, facing an opponent who could out-Nazi the Nazis.

Not many weeks after the débâcle of the Craigard raid, our highest placed source in Russia sent us details of the deal by which North Korea had acquired one of the Russian Typhoon super-submarines. Pyongyang was faced with having to pay over the next forty-nine years for a vessel she had now lost.

Soon, our Korean desk began to collect rumours that were circulating in Pyongyang. Several high officers, from both army and navy, were said to have been shot. There was at first no explanation for this purge. Later it was said that the officers' crime had been to act on their own initiative, without sanction from the government.

What that initiative had involved, none of our agents knew. I suggested that, without revealing any details of the action, our agents should spread the news that 'Western inferiors', as we were called in Pyongyang propaganda, had destroyed North Korea's most expensive piece of equipment, the 'super-sub' kept secret even from her own people. Not the executed officers were to blame, but the unexpected toughness of the Westeners. This ought to shatter a lot of North Korean self-confidence. Our aim should be to weaken the people's confidence in its leadership and their faith in government pronouncements.

So far as I know, stories to this effect were never circulated. What we heard instead was that two men from the British Embassy in Seoul had disappeared.

Not until ten weeks later did the North Koreans announce that they were holding the two, who were to be placed in front of a People's Court on espionage charges. According to the prosecution, the two Britons had violated the frontier to cross from South Korea into the North, where they set about filming military installations. Only the vigilance of the people's sure shield, the invincible Army of the People's Democratic Republic, had put an end to the crimes of the Western inferiors.

Nazis had demonstrated their contempt for other races with the term 'sub-human'. Not a great deal of difference from being dismissed as contemptible 'inferiors'.

The truth about the disappearance of our two men was of course that they had been abducted from South Korea and taken into the North. We all knew what that meant. In due course, after the two had been sentenced to a lifetime in a North Korean labour camp, Pyongyang would offer them in exchange for the four prisoners whom we still held.

Not a word about the landing on Craigard had escaped into the public domain. According to what I heard, the Foreign Office had summoned the North Korean Ambassador and handed him a strong but discreet protest. Repetition of any such hostile action would have the gravest possible consequences. This is what I was told, though to me it seems unlikely that that particular wording was used. 'Gravest possible consequences' is diplomat-speak for war. This, I am sure, is not what we intended. On the other hand, I did not doubt that, as I was also told, the Ambassador was deeply shocked at news of the raid, that he had no idea of what had happened, and that the operation had indeed been kept secret from Pyongyang.

The FO stated Britain's readiness to repatriate the bodies of the dead, if this should be desired, and advised that we held four prisoners who were being treated for wounds. As I understood it, the FO had indicated that the prisoners would be held in the UK until agreement should be reached concerning the level of reparations to be paid by North Korea to the UK. Such reparations would take into consideration the lifetime pensions to be paid to the widows and families of British servicemen killed in the action. The cost of equipment lost (e.g., two motor boats), the provision of an interpreter and other disbursements would also find consideration. Medical treatment to the wounded prisoners would on the other hand not be charged to their own government.

This had been enough for Pyongyang to initiate its tit-for-tat move. The offer to repatriate the dead was not taken up, and the MoD decided to establish a cemetery for them on the island where they had died.

There was no doubt in our minds – I am speaking, besides myself, for Brigadier Dickson, Major Jardine and all other officers on Craigard – that the Korean dead, just as much as our British casualties, were victims of the régime in Pyongyang. Men mentally transmuted into suicides, sent across to the far side of the world to be slaughtered, their families kept in ignorance of where they had gone, what had happened to them, or why.

Highly placed officers were shot not because they had acted on their own initiative, but because the operation had failed and the submarine had been lost.

The rage that I had felt on first seeing one of those raiders had been replaced by a sad, enveloping regret. After all that the world had suffered during the twentieth century, I was appalled that anyone should still imagine that there was something to be gained by violence against another state.

Meanwhile, the prisoner who had lost a hand was earning Naismith's admiration with his positive attitude towards the future. 'I can paint pictures, and draw', he told Millie. 'I can play darts and do fencing'. The man set to thinking of all the pursuits that he could still follow using one hand. Pistol shooting he mentioned, then seemed embarrassed. The army would discharge him, but what sort of work would he find?

Well, that would take care of itself, he was sure. There seemed little that would upset this man.

The lieutenant was of a very different nature. Resentment one could understand in a prisoner, particularly one halfway round the world away from his home. Resentment was not enough for the lieutenant, who was determined to maintain the hostility displayed during the landing. Towards those who were trying to help him he displayed nothing but truculence.

I went unfailingly with Naismith and Millie on the MO's daily visits of inspection. The lieutenant's wounds were healing beyond all expectation. It was entirely thanks to Naismith's efforts and skill that the lieutenant was alive at all.

I do not think that it was naïve of me to have expected the odd expression of thanks to Naismith or to an orderly who changed a dressing. A nod or a slight smile would have been sufficient. The lieutenant, though, remained surly.

As was usual on commando operations, none of the North Koreans was carrying any identification. The FO could therefore notify Pyongyang of the dead only by naming the prisoners and confirming that all others had died.

The three wounded privates gave their names readily enough. Doubtless they were anxious for their families to know that they were alive, even though imprisoned far away. No one at home, of course, had any idea that the men had been in action.

The lieutenant refused to answer any questions. Recorded conversations between the prisoners were no help, since the others addressed their officer only by his rank. By exercise of a little cunning as well as of her natural charm, Millie learned in time from one of the privates that the lieutenant's name was Dong-sun, meaning 'Integrity of the East'. I have no doubt that the man saw it as his mission to live up to this name and am sure that he imagined he was preserving this integrity by his complete refusal to cooperate in even the smallest way with his captors.

We were prepared to allow the prisoners to write home, offering to deliver any letters, after censoring of course, to their Embassy in London for forwarding. As expected, Dong-sun refused this privilege. The others wrote industriously and their letters went in a steady stream to the North Korean Embassy, but I have serious doubts whether any letter was ever sent on to the men's families.

Naismith and his medical orderlies, of course, were uniformed. Millie and I wore our own choice of clothes, and I have wondered many times since whether our civilian dress might not have appeared sinister to Dong-sun, as though we were both the worst kind of secret police officers.

Though I continued to take Millie with me to visit the four men long after daily medical examinations had ceased to be necessary, it proved impossible to break down Dong-sun's reserve. The others would readily enter into harmless conversations with me. Yet whenever I appeared, Dong-sun would bury himself in a book. Even a simple comment on the weather he would treat as though I had asked him to betray his country's most sensitive and valuable secret.

If by such behaviour Dong-sun had hoped to put me off visiting him, he was mistaken. I still looked in on him daily, with Millie as interpreter, of course.

After a year of silence about our two abducted diplomats, Pyongyang told our Ambassador there that it was willing to forego a trial, even on such a grave charge as military espionage. As a gesture of goodwill to the United Kingdom, our men would be released, provided that the United Kingdom was prepared to reciprocate this humanitarian gesture by returning the four soldiers detained by us.

For me it was a poignant moment when Dong-sun and the others were put aboard an airliner for their journey home. Our own two men were already on their way, having taken off an hour earlier. I found the exchange far too evocative of Anna's return to London from incarceration by the KGB.

Headquarters had asked that I should attend at Heathrow, along with Millie and two men from the section that covered the two Koreas. I gathered that I was none too popular with these, being regarded as both an interloper and a glory-hunter.

Odd, how many people rush into resentment and rejection even when facts are before them pointing unequivocally to a contrary conclusion. Headquarters had called me in for the start of this episode. Headquarters thought that I should finish off the job, too. None of it was my idea.

I forbore to offer either of the prisoners my hand, having a strong feeling that Dong-sun would report with glee any apparent fraternizing of his men with a capitalist lackey and imperialist running dog like myself.

Quite apart from the fact that I was relieved at the return of our own innocent diplomats, I was also pleased for the four prisoners to see them on their way home. Yes, even Dong-sun. He might have not the least concept of ordinary courtesy, let alone chivalry, yet he had gone into battle, almost died from his wounds and then been imprisoned on the other side of the world for a year. His suffering, too, deserved some respect.

Otherwise, we should be no better than he was.

XIV

THAT year we had what many people might call a good old-fashioned winter. Our part of Argyll seldom had a massive fall of snow. That year it did. I had always loved the sight of trees balancing an inch or more of snow even on the slenderest of branches. That year I had my fill.

I remembered as a boy hearing someone comment that snow belonged in the country and not at all in the town. Was this, I wondered, one of those commonplace remarks repeated without thought yet taken by the first time listener as evidence of wisdom on the part of the pronouncer?

Whatever the case, I concurred heartily with the sentiment. The whiteness of our gardens and of the hills around had inarguably its own beauty, objectively comparable with the loveliness of those purples, greens, browns and yellows of a Highland summer. Against this, I had the most uncomfortable memories of winters in London and Berlin. A paddling pool of black slush underfoot and underwheel is the price we pay for carpeting the earth with stone, concrete and tar, preventing natural seepage.

That year at home it was a delight to watch the interaction of sun and snow, the unblemished whiteness dying foot by foot. Vanishing from garden, from glen. Retreating yard by yard towards the tops of hills, yet lingering still beneath the summits, as though to say: You can push me so far, but no farther.

All colours of crocus were enlivening the borders beneath wall and hedge, buds of every kind were intimating their appearance.

Along the path that I had cleared with a welcome burst of exercise, the postman brought a letter with a Berlin postmark. It was addressed in a spidery hand with what I still thought of as a proper pen: one with a nib, and ink that flowed without pressure on the paper.

I knew whose hand it was before turning over the envelope. The sender's name on the flap was as familiar as any from my Berlin years. The address, on the other hand, shook me a little, though I suppose that it should not have. It was that of a care home in Spandau.

Tosca was the code name of a woman who had escaped from the Soviet zone of Germany literally on the last train to run from there into the West before the border was closed and walled. I had been Tosca's controller for some years. She had done invaluable work for us by, among other tasks, infiltrating quasi-political groups in West Berlin and identifying Communist agents. My personal relationship with Tosca had always been one of close friendship, to the extent that it was not difficult to recognize how for this woman I had become rather like the son that she had never had.

Anna had met Tosca once, years before, when I had introduced my agent untruthfully as a landlady from whom I had earlier rented a room.

Even at that one short meeting, Anna had sensed the maternal role that Tosca, perhaps unconsciously, was adopting in her relations with me. Ever since, Anna had teased me gently about my 'adoptive mother'. Officially,

Anna knew nothing of the professional relationship between us, and I had no wish to enlighten her. Between Anna and me, Tosca remained, under her real name of course, my 'old landlady'. All the same, I suspect that Anna guessed easily at the truth.

With the collapse of the Wall and the reunification of Germany, strings of agents were paid off, not just in Berlin but throughout Central Europe.

And now here was Tosca, animated, full of ideas and adventure, spirited, indefatigable Tosca, outwardly years younger than her true age, in an old folks' home! What an idiot I was! I should have realized that the years had gone by for Tosca as well as for the rest of us.

Tosca had only recently moved into the Spandau home, and had written requesting a visit from me. What a marvellous idea! Of course it would be splendid to see the old girl again. Though I prepared myself to find Tosca greatly changed and perhaps fragile, I was began to look forward to our meeting with something like joy. We should have a great deal to talk about.

In my Shostakovich bag when I boarded the Berlin flight at Heathrow were several tins of shortbread for the old lady. No duty-free whisky for the chaps at Berlin Station. Not any more. The ban on taking liquids on board had put paid wholesale to such ritualistic courtesies.

Flight attendants – I still thought of them as stewardesses – invariably demonstrated fussy concern as soon as they saw my dot-and-carry method of climbing into an aircraft. I needed no assistance and wanted none. All the same, I had no wish to appear ungrateful, and certainly not brusque. With what I hoped was faultless courtesy, I declined the crew's attentions in the sociable spirit in which these were offered, protesting truthfully that my injuries were not as bad as they appeared. 'You should see the other fellow', I always insisted, and it was true that the Russian whose bullet severed some of my back muscles had himself gone home wounded.

They gave me an aisle seat where I could stretch out my gammy leg. Before the machine began its descent towards Berlin, a stewardess appeared at my elbow, suggesting that I remain seated until all other passengers had alighted. This suited me, since whenever possible I made a practice of waiting until the general rush was over before leaving my seat. Standing and waiting with a case in my hand or at my feet had no appeal for me. I had always wondered at my fellow passengers' eagerness to be on their feet early, when none could leave an aircraft or a railway carriage until the machine was at a halt and doors were opened. Were most people incapable of thinking even a minute or two ahead? Apparently not.

My fellow passengers were the usual mixture of middle-aged couples, laptop-engrossed businessmen, over-made-up women travelling alone and young men in jeans with unruly hair. While these twisted, sidled and bumped their way to the forward exit, I found myself astonished, not for the first time, at the sheer size and bulk of what some people considered to be suitable cabin baggage.

Among its many advantages over the old Tempelhof field, the new Brandenburg Airport had a rail link directly into the heart of the capital.

I decided to ignore this and take a taxi.

The home where Tosca was now resident was situated in a refreshingly green area of Spandau. As we neared the institution I realized that I had forgotten how much farther advanced here would be the burgeoning spring. Even cherry trees already wore their full-dress blossom. I had forgotten, too, how much at home I had always felt in Berlin. I had been at home anywhere in Germany, but more so in Berlin than anywhere else.

It was good to be back.

XV

THE entrance to the care home, through double doors entirely of glass, led into a spacious hall not unlike the lobby of a good class hotel. Sofas and armchairs were scattered about, while massive full length windows permitted a generous view of the outside, green world. Except for one who was asleep, solitary individuals, and some couples, sat enjoying the view of the tree-lined avenue that ran past the home.

Corridors off to either side led to a restaurant and to a small shopping centre. There were two receptionists at the busy desk. One appeared to be deep in explanations to a middle-aged couple, one of whom was doubtless the son or daughter of an inmate. Is that what one called them? Inmates? No. Surely residents would be the correct term.

The second receptionist, who looked barely twenty, asked me to sign a visitors' book. Once I had complied, she gave me instructions for finding Tosca's apartment. That was what the residents had, apparently. Apartments. Every one self-contained and creating the illusion of living in a private block of flats. Nonetheless, medical personnel were on hand round the clock.

A notice board carried a list of the residents who had so far died that month. An inescapable reminder that such homes were the termini in many lives.

As I approached Tosca's apartment, I saw that her door was ajar. I stopped to ring the bell. Before I could reach the button, Tosca called out: 'Come in, Ian'. Clearly, Tosca's hearing was unimpaired. Her voice, though, was weaker than I remembered it. I stepped inside. Tosca was standing beside an armchair, resting a hand on the back of it.

Naturally I had expected to see her aged, but I had not envisaged this amount of change. Her cheeks were sunken, her nose reduced to a point. Eyes that had never been other than lively were now without lustre. She was moving stiffly, too.

Tosca greeted me with her customary embrace and kiss. I kissed her cheek in return, and was relieved to find it soft and warm as ever. From Tosca's appearance, I had feared that she might be hardening away to a living skeleton.

Tosca, I could see, had managed to furnish her apartment with many of the treasured pieces from the old home that, with much effort, she had set up for herself after arriving in the West. Chairs, sideboard and tables, all early 19th century, had made the transition with her. So too, had dozens of photographs, many in silver frames. Propped against a wall in a corner of the room was a walking stick – one of those with a handle shaped to fit a hand.

One notable absentee was Tosca's piano. A grand piano had been the centrepiece of that old home. I had not visited Tosca there until both my early retirement and the end of the Cold War had ended our professional relationship. On those calls, Tosca would play that instrument for hours on end. Beethoven sonatas, Chopin, Schumann, Grieg – it had always been a delight to listen to her, and to watch those supple fingers dancing back and forth, up and down. I knew, too, that it was a pleasure to her to play for someone who so dearly valued the music.

When she had something to report to me in our working days, Tosca's eyes always held a light of steely animation. Her eyes as she looked at me now had something of supplication in them. Whatever Tosca was going to ask, she was begging me to concur. This was certainly a new Tosca.

Almost from my arrival I had found myself sitting, as had been our custom, with coffee and a wedge of gateau.

Tosca waited until the cake had disappeared and I had refused a second piece.

'Do you', she asked, 'consider suicide a sin?'

I knew at once what lay behind the question. 'I consider to be a sin', I answered, 'the arrogance of other people in telling terminally ill folk who have nothing before them but further suffering that they must endure and wait to die naturally. No one should be able to interfere with another's right to end his or her life'.

I had known such a case. A young man, struck down in his early twenties by some ghastly affliction and confined to a wheelchair from then on. One after another, he lost all his movements of limbs and body. Finally, the fellow could move nothing below his neck. Baby-like, he needed round the clock attention from nurses, had to be bottle- and spoon fed, lifted from wheelchair to bed and back again. He had turned forty, had endured this parody of existence for many years and wished to die. His request that he travel to a euthanasia clinic in Switzerland was greeted with expressions of horror by his religious mother. She refused to assist him in any way, condemning him to further years of pointless suffering until one night, mercifully, he died in his sleep.

This episode had infuriated me at the time, and still infuriates me when I think of it now. If this were not unkind, I could wish that the poor man's mother would develop the same infirmity, in order to learn a lesson.

How much difference was there, I wondered, between Nazis who had favoured euthanasia even when it was not wanted or needed, and non-Nazis who opposed it when it was? Either case, by imposing one's will and beliefs on others, meant displaying contempt for one's fellows.

'I had polio when I was three', Tosca revealed. 'I was cured, and was able to do everything as I grew up – dancing, cycling, skiing, mountain-climbing. There was nothing that I couldn't do'.

How well I remembered! Tosca had always been as active as any woman twenty years younger. This is no exaggeration. In the days when she was one of our most valuable agents, we would meet in cafes or occasionally at the opera. It sounds ridiculous, I know, but staff at these establishments frequently seemed to take us for a married couple, though Tosca was twenty years and some months older than myself.

She had never shown not the least lingering sign of having had childhood polio – no limp or anything of that sort. Now, she said, the polio had come back. And she had a walking stick in the corner.

'When polio returns in later life', Tosca explained, 'there is no treatment for it. Not here, not in America. There are about six hundred patients worldwide who have polio for the second time. None of them can be helped'.

'No treatment at all?'

'Nothing. I've lost the use of my left hand. Look'.

I looked. I had not noticed this while she was pouring the coffee, and she had craftily cut the cake before I arrived, but the hand had stiffened into a kind of claw. In addition, her arm appeared to have shrunk. This, I thought, was an illusion, but it suggested that arm and hand together would one day become quite useless. No wonder that the grand piano had gone. There could be no mystery about Tosca's question on suicide If life were going to depart from all four limbs...

Let us, I thought, do some things together while we still can.

'How would it be', I asked, 'if we walked a little – beside the river, perhaps?'

I had never seen a note of apology, or anything like it, in Tosca's eyes. She had never been other than intense and affirmative, almost bursting for action. The gaze she gave me now was full of regret.

'I'm sorry. I can walk only a few steps. Just here in the apartment. I manage to go from chair to kitchen, from bathroom to bed, and that is all. I'm sorry'.

What on earth made the woman feel that she had to apologize? It was I who was sorry. Such a spirit as hers deserved better.

On the way to Tosca's apartment I had seen three or four wheelchairs folded in a corridor alcove.

'Do those wheelchairs outside belong to particular individuals, or are they for anyone to use?'

'They belong to the home. They are for anyone who needs them'.

'How about if I pushed you outside for a while? It's a lovely day'.

'But I don't want you to push me like a lackey'.

'Lackey indeed! What nonsense. Remember how much I owe you from the past. You were my best agent. You'd like to go outside, wouldn't you? See how far the spring has come?'

Though it was a lovely day, as I had said, I nonetheless wrapped a blanket round Tosca's legs. We went round the paths of an adjacent park. We went to the river, followed it along until it broadened out into the Spandauer See, and regretted that we had brought nothing with which to feed the birds.

It was apparent that Tosca enjoyed this outing. No less evident was that she found it in some way demeaning, for me as much as for her. It was banal. Even our conversation had become banal.

Her legs were worse than she had originally let me know. 'I lay down on the bed all day until you arrived', she admitted, 'so as to save up the energy I needed to stand, open the door and organize the coffee. One day, if I don't take even that amount of exercise, I shall be confined to bed round the clock'.

And this had been a woman who could bustle her way through a crowd like an electric current leaping for the nearest piece of copper.

I stayed for a week, wheeling Tosca out each day. Though I tried to find original routes to follow, we ended always at the river and then at a café where we could sit at an outside table. There we watched the passenger boats, washed down oversweet confectioners' creations with unsweetened black coffee and reminded each other of narrow escapes we had had during the Cold War. Popeye, the most successful Communist double agent, had cost the lives of several of our people, yet here we were now, talking of those days as though they had been, if not romantic, then at least enjoyable.

Before I flew home, I told Tosca: 'I have only one request. Don't do anything before you have told me that you have made a decision. I shall come and help in any way that I can'.

What I meant was: Even if have to wheel you out to my car and drive you myself to Switzerland and to the euthanasia clinic.

XVI

EVERY weekend after that, I telephoned Tosca for a progress report on her worsening lameness. After two months, there were signs that both arms were becoming useless. I flew to Germany again.

We took off in dull weather, landed at Brandenburg in brilliant sun. I collected my Shostakovich bag and headed this time for a car hire firm.

'Is that you, Ginger?' The voice was familiar, though not instantly recognizable. I turned.

'It is you. By Jove, I never thought to see you here again. What's the matter? Can't keep away from the place?'

It would have to be Sheridan. The one man whom, during my time at Berlin Station, I had never liked. And also the one man insubordinate enough to use that particular epithet about my hair.

What was Sheridan doing here? Surveillance, no doubt. It would serve him right if through the attention he was giving to me he lost sight of whatever his prey might be. It could be amusing to know how he would explain that one in his report.

My mischievous side tempted me to delay Sheridan by starting an unnecessary and prolonged conversation. Good sense countered that I could not sabotage one of Berlin's operations, however trivial it was. Good sense won.

I dismissed Sheridan with 'Mustn't keep you. Nice to have seen you again', and went in to collect my car. I dislike hypocrisy, and despise myself whenever formalities demand that I use it.

The hire car had a special purpose. Would Tosca like a journey into the past?

We took a wheelchair, folded, in the boot, and drove straight to Tosca's home town. The house in which she had grown up had given way to a lifeless block of flats in the Soviet style. Her old school, on the other hand, was still standing. Tosca gazed at it from outside the gate for some minutes, then directed me to the cemetery where her family lay interred. After the names of her mother and father, Tosca's own name and birth date had, I noticed, been added already to one of the newer gravestones.

Was this a recent addition, I wanted to know.

'Oh no. I had it put on at the same time as I ordered the stone for my parents'.

Flower-laying done, we headed back to Spandau. Tosca's legs were worsening, and she doubted that she would much longer be able even to move around in her apartment. 'I've got the papers for the suicide', she told me. By this, I assumed that she meant forms from the clinic in Switzerland.

The subject was not mentioned again, by either of us. I did not wish to be the one to raise it, and should speak on the matter only if Tosca did.

She didn't, and I took this as a heartening sign that her lameness, though worsening, was not yet making life unbearable.

By this time, spring was imparting a feeling of merging into early summer. Every day we drove to a different destination in the countryside around Berlin. As far as possible, we ate at village restaurants that had outside tables. I would push Tosca up to a table in her chair, and we would linger with our reminiscences until a dipping sun began to take the warmth out of the day. On these excursions Tosca displayed again the old vigorous personality that had served us so well and that I hated to see fettered by a failing body.

On the day that I was to fly home, we parted with the usual embrace and Tosca's assurance that she was going to avoid becoming bedridden for as long as possible.

That's my girl, I thought. With Tosca, how could it be otherwise?

At Brandenburg Airport I handed back the hire car and checked through my bag. Was it possible, I wondered as I sat waiting for the call to my flight, to distinguish one airport boarding lounge from another? Motel rooms look all the same. Railway stations, too, have a way of resembling each other. It was certainly true that as I sat in the boarding lounge at Brandenburg I could have believed myself waiting to embark at an airport serving any one of a dozen cities.

Not that I would allow my surroundings to intrude on my thoughts. As usual when I had time to kill, I pulled out a crossword book. To be frank, I buried myself in crosswords as a way of testing my continuing mental fitness. I had known two brilliant men whose mental powers had collapsed completely with little prior warning. Such a state was, I understood, irreversible. If this were to happen to me, I hoped that I should have some indication in advance. When I could no longer tackle the cryptic crosswords, that would be warning enough. Another check on my powers that I practised was to do long division in my head.

For Tosca, matters were completely the other way round. Her mind was as sharp as ever. It was her body that was failing.

The London flight was called, we all rose and began to form a line to hand in our boarding passes and show our passports at the exit desk. I thought nothing of the two policemen who were standing behind the girl from the airline. Not until, that is, one of them reached forward to take my passport from the girl's hand.

'You are Ian Baxter Greig?'

I affirmed it.

'Would you come with us, please?' The man was politeness itself. Thoughtful, too. 'See to it that Mr Greig's baggage is not loaded', he instructed the airline girl.

Taking a later flight was not going to incommode me overmuch. What on earth, though, was going on?

They kept me waiting in the back of a car until my bag had been retrieved and stowed in the boot.

If I had had the least idea that I was being arrested on suspicion of some offence, I should have kicked up a fuss. This, though, was evidently something different. Someone wanted to talk to me. In the old days, cooperation with our West German intelligence counterparts, men of the Bundesnachrichtendienst, was sporadic rather than on a day-to-day basis. The contacts we maintained were not close, but they were good. It was not difficult to imagine that, my name having cropped up from airport surveillance, someone from those days wanted to see me. Whoever it was, he must know that I was long out of the Service. If he were hoping to milk me for information, he was liable to be out of luck. He surely did not want to recruit me for a special job or jobs.

These were the questions in my mind as we drove at a brisk pace to police headquarters in Potsdam.

The ground floor. An ordinary interview room. No window. A simple table, plain chairs. Nothing else. I sat where I was invited, with my back to the door. A uniformed policeman stood in a corner behind me.

I heard the men come in, rose automatically and turned. I found myself looking into a pair of blue eyes that were regarding me with close interest. They were set in a reddish round face that it would not be unfair to describe as chubby. The body beneath was, by contrast, not at all chubby. Strong and well-built, yes. Chubby, no. The man wore a medium grey, well fitting suit. His dark brown hair was brushed flat, with not a hair astray at the parting. I assessed his age as barely fifty.

I reached out a hand, saw momentary hesitation in the newcomer's eyes. He cleared the expression quickly and gave me a brief handshake. It was the sort of grip that I like – firm and brisk. Unlike the usual practice, he did not give his name.

Behind him came a second, younger man who walked in a semicircle round the far side of the other. It

261

looked as though he wished to avoid my handshake. This man was younger – early thirties, I thought – slim but evidently strong. He carried a brown card folder. Neither man was someone I recognized from my Service days in Berlin.

The older man took his seat directly opposite me, the younger on his right.

It was the older one who spoke. He opened my passport, asked me to confirm my identity and date of birth.

'What was your relationship with Frau X-Y Z?' Naturally, he used Tosca's real name, hyphenated Christian names and all.

'We had worked together some years ago, and remained friends after we retired'.

'You both retired together? But Frau Z was twenty years older than you'.

'I retired early to look after my wife, who had contracted a fatal illness'.

'And your wife – she is dead?'

'Yes'.

'I am sorry'.

'Thank you'.

'You did not think of resuming work after your wife had died?'

'I wasn't sure that the work would be there for me again'.

'Yes. You had a very exclusive job, Mr Greig'.

'As doubtless so do you'.

'You gave up work to look after your wife. You saw that as your mission, so to speak. Did you also see it as your mission to look after Frau Z?'

'All I have done is take her for...' I paused. I did not like a thought that had come to me. 'Are you speaking of Frau Z in the past tense?'

'In what tense should I speak of her?'

'In the present, of course'.

The older man made a small gesture. His colleague opened an envelope and slid a photograph across the table towards me.

It was Tosca, and it was not Tosca. A section of plastic bag sucked into the gaping mouth. Drawn, too, onto her glazed, unseeing eyes. The nose, newly pointed with age, now a parody of the child's face pressed against a confectioner's window. The bag, stretched and taut, taped heavily round the neck.

Another blunt instrument, if not as original as Anna's.

XVII

I HAD not felt such anger since seeing Anna's condition when she returned from the attentions of the KGB.

Whoever had done this had certainly worked fast. I began to calculate backwards. There could not have been much more than an hour and a half between my having kissed Tosca goodbye and my being picked up at the airport. Had the killer tipped off the police?

Well, that wasn't important. Any member of staff, bringing in a meal or on any other errand, would have discovered her.

I looked up to see blue eyes in a chubby round face regarding me with some intensity. 'Is there anything that you want to tell us about this?'

'I was hoping', I told him, 'that you could tell me something'.

'You don't seem very upset'. This was the younger man. 'I thought you cared about the woman'.

What the hell did he know? Inside I was seething, not just with anger but with sorrow. I had had plenty of practice in controlling my emotions, had often been mistakenly accused of callousness because of refusing to give way.

I looked at the fellow and was on the point of giving him my tongue when the older man spoke up. 'Mr Greig is trained not to show his feelings, isn't that so, Mr Greig? He can tell us lie after lie and we shall never be able to read in his face that they are all lies. We are dealing with an expert'.

I suppose that after an opening encounter like that no suspect would have any right to complain. Police cards had been laid plainly on the table. Anything I said would not be believed. They had made this unequivocally clear, and I should not be able to complain of entrapment or any such deception.

Police had all the answers.

My fingerprints were all over Frau Z's apartment, but none was on the plastic bag or the tape used to kill her.

Naturally I had worn gloves. That just confirmed that the murder was premeditated.

But no gloves were found in my baggage.

Of course not. I had dumped those in a waste bin somewhere between the crime scene and the airport. I was well trained in that style of silent murder, wasn't I? Hands of victim well taped together first, then the bag that could not be pulled off.

I had no motive.

Oh yes I had. The doctor at the care home confirmed it. Frau Z's will was witnessed by himself and another member of staff. To the doctor she had revealed that she was leaving everything to me.

I had not had the faintest idea of such a thing.

No? Strange. This was a second will, made just after my earlier visit. It replaced the previous bequests to charity. Frau Z would surely have told me.

She hadn't.

They had only my word for that. What's more, the amount of the legacy was considerable. Frau Z had savings sufficient to finance her stay at the home – an expensive one – for another fifteen years. Work out for yourself what her murder now leaves in the account. Oh yes, I had a motive all right.

And so on.

I made a statement as they insisted, but it was not the one they wanted. I described my last hours with Tosca and how, when I had left her, she was 'alive and, though not entirely well, at least cheerful'.

They left it at that for the day. They fed me well, I must admit, and once I had switched off my pain and fury at Tosca's murder I slept decently on their hard detention cell bed. They could not know it, but thin mattresses of that kind were what I preferred.

There was no shortage of coffee next morning, and there was no question that being locked up at Spandau was far more comfortable than the same experience at Service headquarters in London. I had quite a chat with the uniformed officer who had charge of the cells. The man had twice been to Scotland following his football team in European competitions, and was enthusiastic about the passion generated by Scottish fans. It was not the first such conversation that I had had in Germany. Like music, football really is an international language.

Not until late morning did the football fan fetch me for more questioning. He did not take me to an interview room, but directly to the office of the detective with the chubby face.

No colleague of his was present to witness all that I said. In his place, a tape recorder would be running under the desk.

So far as I know, British police officers do not have their names displayed on their desks. But as the Germans themselves say, in other countries there are other practices. The name on this desk was Kommissar (Inspector) Hitzler.

I remembered that the inspector had forborn to state his name when he took my hand the day before. Though I was trying to keep all expression out of my face, I fear that I took a second look at the nameplate just to make sure.

'I have heard all the jokes', the inspector assured me. 'Please, sit down'. From a folder on his desk, he took papers stapled together. He looked at me and took his time reading them through. I was supposed to be worrying about what further evidence he was going to produce against me. Having to wait in silence was intended to put me more and more on edge.

Surely the man knew that I was proof against that sort of tactic. He had already indicated that he knew of my occupation during all the years that I had lived in Berlin.

When he reached the end of his reading, Hitzler fixed his eyes on mine. 'You mentioned nothing about Frau Z's desire to commit suicide. Why was that?'

'I considered it irrelevant once she was dead'.

'Irrelevant? You could have used it as an excuse. You were fulfilling Frau Z's heartfelt wish'.

'But I didn't kill her'.

'So you say. The prosecutor's office is certain to take a different view'.

'People can take any view they like'.

'You know of course that assisted suicide is illegal in Germany. There is no advantage in being convicted of assisting a suicide rather than of any other form of murder. That is no doubt why you did not mention it'.

'I don't remember planning on being convicted of anything – least of all any form of murder. Furthermore, you will have found in Frau Z's apartment a form from a euthanasia clinic in Switzerland. That is how you know what was in her mind, but at the same time you must realize how pointless it would have been for me to kill her. All I had to do was drive her to Switzerland'.

'Driving Frau Z to the euthanasia clinic in Switzerland would make you an accessory. That may not be murder, but it is the next thing to it. Even if Frau Z were to have flown to Switzerland, if you just telephoned for a taxi to take her to the airport, even that would make you an accessory and liable to years inside. Of course you covered up what you had done'.

'Rubbish, Herr Hitzler. Holding me is just nonsensical. Somebody killed her, but logically it must have been someone who didn't know about her suicide plan'.

In this I was completely wrong. With or without the killer knowing, he would have killed her just the same.

XVIII

THEY kept me in custody for a further four days. Each morning I was taken along to Hitzler to see whether I would add to, or change anything in, my statement. They offered to bring in someone from the British Consulate, but I told them to forget it.

Tosca's body had been found by a staff member delivering tea almost as soon as I had left the home. Staff had been grilled and checked thoroughly, and there was no suspicion of any kind to be found against anyone. I remained the only suspect, and expected every day to be taken before an examining magistrate, who would determine whether there was a *prima facie* case for me to answer.

On the fifth morning, I was woken early and taken out to an unmarked police car. A uniformed officer on either side, I was driven to Tosca's funeral in her home town, now happily released from the deadening hand of Moscow ideology. This, I told myself, cannot be the usual proceeding. Since when were murder suspects allowed to pay their respects at the graves of their victims?

The day was dull. During every minute of the service I expected the clouds to empty their watery burdens onto us. This did not happen. At the conclusion I was allowed to empty a small shovelful of earth onto the coffin of this dear friend. Looking down at the brass-furnished oak reposing at the foot of its man-made abyss, I swore that when I was finally freed, whoever had killed Tosca would have me to fear as well as the law.

We arrived back at Spandau in the early evening. Instead of being returned to my cell, as I expected, I was taken once more to Hitzler. As I entered his sanctum with my escort, the inspector rose. He leaned over his desk, hand outstretched. 'My congratulations. We have an eye-witness to a man entering Frau Z's apartment via the balcony, and that man was not you'.

That witness must have come forward yesterday. They already knew that their case against me was collapsing when they allowed me out to the funeral.

I had forgotten that Tosca's apartment had glass doors opening onto a balcony. Outside were a lawn, walkways and a screen of tall evergreens. I had had the idea of putting Tosca in a chair out on the balcony once summer weather was there. Since I had been able to better this by taking her out in a car, an occasion for this had simply not arisen.

'The time fits in perfectly', Hitzler went on. 'Just a few minutes after you left for the airport – as confirmed by the receptionist at the home, who logged you out'.

'Have you got the fellow?'

'Not yet, but we shall. The main thing for now is that suspicion is lifted from you. You can go. How was the funeral, by the way?'

'Like all funerals. Not jolly, but at least everything went off without any hitches'.

Hitzler stretched out his hand again. 'I apologize for having detained you. There really was no one else at that time'.

'I know. You were just doing your job. If I had been in your position...' If I had been in his position, I should have paid more attention to the suicide papers from Switzerland, but I did not say this.

They gave me back my bag and offered to drive me to an hotel.

Letting me go like this did seem a little precipitate, if all they had so far was a witness but no evidence. It was impossible not to feel that I was being treated better than the ordinary murder suspect because of who I was and what they knew about me. In any case, if they wanted me again, they could easily have me picked up. These days there was something called a European arrest warrant.

There remained a massive problem: what motive could Tosca's mystery visitor have had for killing her?

Hitzler had realized his error in homing in on me – but how was he going to set about finding the real killer and proving the case against him?

The eye witness turned out to be a boy of eight years. He had been playing in the park just outside the home's perimeter fence and looking through beneath the tall evergreens that lined the boundary on the inside. According to what he told his mother some days later, he had seen what he described as a 'Chinaman' wearing 'ordinary clothes' hoisting himself up over the parapet of Tosca's balcony. A few minutes later, the 'Chinaman' had emerged the same way and disappeared round a corner of the building.

On further questioning of the boy, it appeared that the 'ordinary clothes' consisted of a light grey suit. The boy's mother had fetched him home shortly thereafter, and was able to calculate the time of his sighting as very close to the moment I had left for the airport.

Did I know of a Chinaman who had any connection at all with Frau Z? I did not. I did know of a Korean who would naturally be taken by a child for Chinese. Not relevant, though. There could be no conceivable connection with Tosca.

I booked into an hotel and rang a telephone number that I had not called in years.

It was answered by Hanson, an officer who, last time we had met, had been at the start of his career with Berlin Station. He was now practically a veteran, confident and level-headed.

'I'd like to buy you a drink', I told him. This translated as: I need to meet you, either to offer information or to request assistance.

'Fine, old boy'. Hanson was wide awake. 'The poet's, in an hour?'

'See you'.

'The poet's' could have been Schiller's Bar, but it wasn't. It was the Hotel Erato, taking its name from the old Greek muse of lyric poetry. This establishment's principal virtue was that it had a good bar with plenty of room for sitting well away from others.

I took the usual precautions on my way there. Skipping in and out of the great KdW department store by different doors. Two taxis in opposing directions, neither going anywhere near the Erato. I finished the last stage on foot, and still was there before Hanson.

I stood at the bar with my whisky until Hanson came in. Tall, with dark hair showing a first tendency to recede, Hanson had put on a noticeable amount of weight since we had last met. I could see nevertheless that his recent additions were mostly muscle rather than flab. He wore a dark blue pin striped suit, evidently off the peg, and a dark red tie. Hanson was doing his best to appear nondescript, and succeeding fairly well.

'By George', he said. 'I haven't seen you in ages. How's business?'

'Pretty slack', I told him. 'What with this recession biting everywhere, people just don't have the spare cash in their pockets any more'.

'Don't I know it! You've practically got to pull an arm off the average Joe before he'll part with any of his hard-earned'. Hanson looked round. 'Here, let's go and find a seat and you can tell me all about it'.

We settled in armchairs in a far corner where we could face outwards and keep well in sight anyone who might be coming our way.

'I knew you were here', Hanson told me.

Sheridan had spotted me at the airport. I imagined that he hadn't been able to wait to spread the news.

'Sheridan's convinced that you've been brought back in to take over somebody or other's job'.

'It's personal', I admitted, 'though it does tie in with an official job that I did recently'.

'Involving?'

'North Korea has an embassy here now, I take it?'

'Pretty new, of course. Haven't myself crossed swords with any of them yet'.

'All I need to know is whether they have someone there called Dong-sun'.

'I'll find out'.

He did. Hanson called me at my hotel late on the following morning. 'Same again?'

Once more I was in the Erato's bar before Hanson turned up. He placed a photograph on the table. 'Dong-sun'.

I drew in a sharp breath. 'That's the chap'.

'Military attaché'.

I all but laughed. The man did not have the age, the rank or the experience for such a posting. Doubtless, though, he had been given a fast track promotion. But why? The raid on Craigard could have brought him no kind of credit at all.

Hanson saw my amusement. 'A cousin, apparently, of the Supreme Leader. It seems that he's regarded as some kind of monumental hero for having survived goodness knows how many wounds, though where he picked them up no one has any idea...'

No, I thought. And he's as tough and fanatical as they come.

'He's the chap Sheridan was keeping an eye on at the airport. Meeting some bigwig who was flying in'.

And not alone, I realized. He must have put someone on my tail from that moment on.

My arrival had been a gift to him.

XIX

WHAT sort of a mentality was it, I wondered, that instead of just killing me, could think of killing someone obviously dear to me and leaving me in the frame?

Of course, this was mere rhetorical speculation. I knew the answer well enough. It was a sadist's mentality, the sort that had animated SS guards in the death camps and Gestapo men at number 8, Prinz Albrecht Strasse, not so very far from where Hanson and I were sitting. Anyone who thought that sort of thing to have been expunged in 1945 was a victim of the naïvest form of self-deception. He or she will obviously not have been following the news in his or her own lifetime.

It must have been a pretty thoroughgoing surveillance that Dong-sun had put on to me. His man had struck more or less as soon as I had left Tosca.

Had Dong-sun assumed that Tosca was a relative of mine? Either way, he had caused me enough pain to satisfy the most sadistic need for revenge.

He would have had the pleasure of seeing me put away, too, but for chance and an eight-years-old boy.

I had to assume that since my release by the police Dong-sun had put his tail back onto me. I spent the rest of that day, after I left Hanson, thinking and remembering, remembering and thinking.

Next morning I left the hotel after breakfast and strolled along to the river. It took me no more than five or six minutes to spot my tail. I walked alongside the river for about an hour, out and back. Along the way I took particular note of the movements of the passenger boats that plied on the waters.

Next morning, too, I walked to the river. This time, having reached the bank I settled onto a bench and made it apparent that I was in no hurry to resume my walk.

While he used his mobile phone my tail hid, or thought that he was hiding, behind a tree.

Dong-sun joined him much sooner than I thought would be possible. I remained seated for some minutes more, then rose slowly as if stiff, stretched a little and began to stroll along the water's edge.

I reached the pier where the boat trips started, stopped and read the notice displayed. I looked at my watch as though uncertain, let it be seen that I had made up my mind and walked on board the vessel.

These river boats, broad in the beam, sat low in the water. Having to pass under a number of road bridges, they had flat roofs with no superstructure.

I bought myself a schnapps and took a seat at a window. There were not many passengers. I did not look round, and so sensed rather than saw Dong-sun taking his place several rows behind me, towards the stern. The tail he had put on me was not with him.

A crude assassin, I knew, would have seated himself either beside or directly behind me, and not used his knife until on the point of disembarking. Dong-sun would be anything but crude. Until the time came, he was keeping well away from me.

I had a memory of a trip on one of these river boats. It had been many years ago, and I had never forgotten it. Nothing had happened on that occasion. I had merely been given a glimpse of a possibility. I could call up the images of the moment whenever I liked. Truth to tell, I did not like to.

Timing would be everything, if I were not only to escape Dong-sun but also make him pay for the cowardly murder of the helpless Tosca.

I kept an intense watch on everything that we passed along the banks. At the critical moment I rose and sauntered between the rows of seats towards the stern. I should have only this one chance. Everything depended on my having chosen the moment correctly. Too soon would make it easy for Dong-sun. Too late would spoil my own opportunity altogether.

There was a small open deck at the stern, reached by a couple of steps.

I passed outside into the fresh air, and turned to stand looking towards our bow. Dong-sun followed me. He was fixing me with a look of hatred. A knife appeared in his hand. He came up the first step, then the second.

His timing was perfect. So, in a second or two, would mine have to be.

Dong-sun was concentrating his attention on me, staring fixedly towards where I stood at the stern.

He drew back the arm with the knife and made to step forward. I have no doubt that he thought a quick heave of my body over the stern would be simplicity itself.

The boat reached a road bridge. I watched fascinated as the underside of the bridge swept towards us across the flat roof of the boat with what looked like only three or four inches of clearance.

We both stood higher than the roof.

Dong-sun, facing sternwards, saw nothing coming. His head, swept off cleanly by the iron framework of the bridge, hit me in the midriff with a thump. The weight of the impact surprised me, but I could waste no time in wondering.

The military attaché's head bounced off me on to the deck, and I ducked with it to watch the bridge pass well over mine.

EPILOGUE

To be honest, I did not want to write another word. So far as I am concerned, my story is told.

It's the publisher's fault. They are all the same. Always have this idea that a book should have so-and-so many thousand words in it.

I do not share this view. I believe that what is said is the important thing, not how many words a person takes to say it.

You have probably heard the story about Mozart and the nobleman. The high born gentleman commissioned a piece of some sort from the composer. When it was completed, Mozart gave his patron a first performance. 'Very nice', he was told, 'but too many notes, Herr Mozart. Too many notes'.

How many books have I read – and I bet you have, too – about which you would like to tell the author: Too many words, Mr So-and-so, too many words'.

Say what you have to, and shut up, I say.

Surely there is nothing wrong with that.

What I find egregious are split infinitives, hanging participles, carelessness with pronouns and poor syntax. Brevity is fine.

All the same, while my publisher and I have been arguing about this, one small piece of information has come to my notice. I might as well pass it on, and that will add a few more words to the total that some people (though not I) seem to think makes a book either better or worse.

North Korea has, so I understand, abandoned the costly business of 'tuning' the amygdalae of its élite soldiers. The unofficial Craigard venture proved only that blindness to danger blinds men to common sense, as well. It seems that the operation results in far too many functions of the brain becoming bypassed, producing the robot-like behaviour of armies in bygone centuries. Up to and including Napoleonic battles, when firepower was so much weaker, men could stand and face the enemy openly, trusting their lives to luck. Not any more. The soldier confronted by today's weapons needs to be able to think on many levels, including recognizing when to duck.

With those last words, incidentally, I intend no slighting reference to Dong-sun. Those who knew Tosca will agree that he deserved no sympathy, but I do not believe in making fun of an enemy. Not even of such a latter-day Nazi in a Communist coat.

As it happened, I had to face no awkward questions over his death. Officialdom saw it as a ghastly accident to a man unfamiliar with the river, its boats and bridges.

I simply walked back inside the vessel, took a place quietly towards the stern and disembarked at the bow when the boat next stopped. I hid the blood I had on me by folding my jacket over an arm and carrying it so as to obscure my abdomen.

I was back home in Argyll within a day and a half. Just in time to enjoy the summer that had decided to set in.